TORPOR

Jerry L. Crawford

Torpor

ISBN 978-0-9967583-1-4

Produced in the United States of America
www.skyebridgepublishing.com
editor@editingpenandpublishing.com

For my beloved children
Mitchell L. Crawford
Vali Elizabeth Crawford and
Keli Annalee Crawford-Truckey

Lasting gratitude to D.A. Sarac for her gifted
talent in bringing this publication to fruition.

Special appreciation to Frank Gagliano,
"Red" Shuttleworth, Edward EmanuEl,
and early readers Keli and Paul Truckey, Terry
Miller, Dan Slobig, Jack Wright, and John Bailiff.

A Monk was pursued by a ravenous tiger. The Monk came to the edge of a cliff. At the edge of the precipice, lovely berries were ripe. The Monk plucked one, ate it, and said, "How sweet it is."
—Anonymous proverb

TORPOR: Suspended animation. A state of suspended physical power or activities.

Contents

FOREWORD

The set up is this: Code Jen, ace female interrogator of the FBI, and heroine of this unique page turner, interrogates Wolf West, an American leader of a USA ISIS terror group. Even while handcuffed to a table in the overly air-conditioned FBI interrogation room, Wolf—and his outside group of terrorists—are plotting an attack on the U.S. Jen's job is to uncover the attack before it takes place.

These massive interrogation scenes are central to this first novella by Jerry L. Crawford, a noted playwright, actor, stage director, reviewer of films, and baseball maven. And they have the energy of stage play scenes: "You're too fucking gorgeous to be tough enough for this assignment. Wolves eat sheep, honey." Just one line in a spit-in-her-face long speech from handcuffed Wolf's first encounter with Jen. Playwright Crawford has Jen spit back in her own long-driving speech that ends with, "One of us WILL win. You will tell me what I want to know. You may not even know you've told me, but you will."

Each character in each mounting-in-intensity interrogation scene, and in range of rage, intellect, references, articulation, game playing, strategies, humor and charismatic energy, holds her/his own in the battle as the stakes are raised. These often violent, often dialectical—pressured, stage-play verbal confrontations mount in even more intensities and move to physical life-and-death confrontations, and to a violent conclusion.

The entire novella's narrative is written in the present tense. As one watches a performance of a dramatic script, moment to moment, in the present, the *Torpor* reader is never ahead of the moment. Even when the story turns to narrative mode and we get internal points of view from each character—not just from Jen—we absorb the moment, the comment, the epiphany—as each drops in—again, never ahead of that moment. Later, of course, when all hell breaks loose (twists, turns, surprises and betrayals), the novella moves into cinematic action mode. Skillfully done. Figures. Crawford writes insightful film reviews under the byline Yooper Critic for a select mailing list (I'm proud to be on it). The stagings of the action scenes outside the interrogation rooms are cinematic nail biters. The novella's twists and turns bring Jen to a point where she has to devise a weapon to save her life. Crawford the playwright digs back to one of his own favorite plays to find the perfect method for Jen's survival. The play is "Rock and a Soft Place." From the play's preface we learn that, "Based upon 'special op' training I experienced during my two years of active duty. . .how to use special weapons to kill 'targets' silently by striking a 'soft place' on the target."

So. A former play, informed by Crawford's actual army training, gets Jen to improvise a weapon that will astonish you. But will it work here?

Wolf is a ruthless, brilliant, arrogant, articulate, full-of-dazzling-wordplay villain who, in his warped dialectic, often brilliantly analyzes the madness in the world that one might reluctantly agree with. He has the attraction and *tour de force* energy that literary villains often have; and Jen, on some level, is attracted to this attraction.

She is also grateful to Wolf, I think, for reversing the hummingbird lethargy (torpor) that Jen found herself in, in the very first paragraph, in the elevator, as it descended to the fateful Wolf/Jen first confrontation.

Even as Wolf baits her from the very start and throughout, Jen re-finds her own charisma, brilliance, toughness, and is able to discharge a tsunami of language and ideas to swamp Wolf's hurricane of warped dogma. She's disciplined, shrewd, arrogant, tough, intellectual—can volley back history, politics, literature, sports stats, and just about any obscurity that Wolf throws at her to try to rattle her. And, in her inner assessment moments, the old energy is back as she nails her opponent.

Throughout the novella, we are constantly aware—and believe—because her courage is dramatized—that Jen has balls. Lucky for us she is on our side.

Frank Gagliano
Playwright/Librettist/Novelist
www.gaglianoriff.com
Pittsburgh, November 2015

CHAPTER ONE

Feathers and Fur

As the tiny elevator descends five floors beneath the marbled main level of the Hoover Building housing the Federal Bureau of Investigation, Code Jen is thinking about hummingbirds. *How can a bird hovering in suspended animation with helicopter wings save energy? How can it fly backward?* The old lift jerks to a halt. The door opens noisily, very slowly. As she steps into the narrow hall lit by a dull yellow bulb, Code Jen buttons her tailored, dark blue jacket over a beige silk blouse and moves smartly left toward the Interrogation Room.

The damp musky odor of the hall is warm, but she knows the room will be icy. Her long dark brown hair bounces in its ponytail on her slender back. Approaching the metal door she slows her gait. Tall at five-foot-nine inches, her sharp, dark blue trousers nip at her black shoes with leather strings. Well toned by daily workouts at the Bureau's Fitness Center, her arms and legs are appropriately muscled. She wears subtle makeup, a simple Timex watch, and small, silver earrings. On the middle finger of her right hand is a man's Mason ring with an expensive diamond once worn by her father. She stops, opens the file marked "Confidential," and reviews the photo of the man labeled simply as "Wolf West." He is probably in his late forties, she surmises, though no official birth date is known. In the photo he has a full mustache and surprisingly no beard. The hair is short, already full of silver streaks, matching the mustache. He sports a grin, which appears to her blue eyes as a smirk. His eyes are dark blue. Stung by Chief Gordon's recent, negative evaluation of her, which noted that she could be hyper-enthusiastic and aggressive, she steels herself for the encounter with the prisoner inside the room. The man within bears more than a dangerous reputation. He is considered to be "evil incarnate." Jen had scoffed at that cliché when offered by Chief Gordon, earning her a rebuke.

Jen slides her identification-coded card through the entry slot. A loud buzz accompanies the door opening automatically. Jen enters and shivers. The temperature is almost cool enough to see breath.

The space has one bare table except for a pair of handcuffs locked securely to its surface. A straight-backed, wooden chair stands on either side of the table. A bright white bulb caged in wire lights the room. On one wall is a window with a one-way viewing glass. The air is pristine, clear, a relief from that hallway. Wolf West sits locked in the handcuffs. His hands are not large, but dark, perhaps tanned, riddled with scars from old wounds. The man's eyes are a darker blue than seen in his photo. His face is tan, almost the shiny leather of an old saddle. His hair is unkempt, greasy, needing a shampoo. As in the photo, it is dark brown but heavily streaked with gray, as is his mustache. The orange jump suit is soiled to a dulled yellow.

He smiles at her. "I'm Irish. You?"

Startled, Jen does not respond, taking the other chair. They look at one another in silence, both expressionless. At the live appearance of his photo-familiar smirk, she speaks. "Why do they call you Wolf West?"

He laughs loudly, stopping abruptly. "Ask them, Sugar Tits. My name is Joe Smith."

Now she laughs. "Alias for Samuel T. Worth? May I call you Sam?"

He scoffs. "Only if I can call you Sugar Tits. 'Wolf' serves. Use it."

"My name to you is simply Code Jen."

He laughs again. "Jasus H. Christ! Ok, Jen. I refuse to talk to anyone labeled 'Code.' Is Jen your real name or is that part of the Code shit?"

She resists an urge for combat. "Wolf West because you were caught in Nevada?"

"It's your file not mine. Do you always answer questions with questions?"

"We'll leave it as Wolf and Jen," she firmly announces opening the file.

Before she can get down to business, Wolf pulls against the cuffs, ripping off a torrent of words.

"Before you unleash your questions formed as warps, turns, falters, and dead ends, I have a few questions of my own. Have you spent more time hospitalized or institutionalized? Were you born in Los Angeles, Las Vegas, Des Moines, Chicago, Baton Rouge, Cleveland, Pittsburgh, Boston, New York, London, Paris, Berlin, Moscow, Cairo, Baghdad, Erbil, Kabul, or Chadron? How thoroughly were you trained? Have you used it in the field? Who paid for your smartphone, who do you sleep with, who feeds you, is there pathology in your marriage or are you divorced? Don't let silences accumulate."

Stunned, Jen stares at him. She merely blinks, caught off guard. He resumes.

"Cat got the ol' tongue, eh? Do you have a Miley Tongue Way Out? Are your lyrics aimed at a lowest common denominator audience? Don't spare me for fear some fuse would blow in my brain from exasperation over au currant celebrity-hubris. JASUS SYPHILITIC CHRIST, SAY SOMETHING, WOMAN!"

Jen remains silent. Her thoughts return to hummingbirds—she knows now what torpor feels like. He rails on.

"If the stupid FBI sends you as Chief Interrogator, the main question arises. Have you ever, even belatedly, arrived at the truth? About anything or anyone? You're too fucking gorgeous to be tough enough for this assignment. Wolves eat sheep, honey. You strike me already as the cunning architect of your own collapsed psychophysical structure. You and your government are tragedy-clad. You're a raven-haired, sickly thirty-some, no doubt with a song about the damaged and the wrecked. Women should wean themselves off the absurdity of victimhood. You are a stain against silence."

Jen inhales deeply and asks, "Would you like a Coca-Cola?"

Wolf howls with cackling laughter then relaxes. "Well done, Jen. You know you're no match, so treat me to a soda and leave me the fuck alone."

Jen smiles softly. "Diet or leaded?"

Wolf snaps suddenly with sincere menace. "Zero." Jen rises, exiting. "Zero it is."

In the hall she leans back against the door, inhaling deeply. Wolf is far more than she expected. She walks around the corner finding Inspector Chief Pat Gordon staring through the one-way window at Wolf. Gordon frowns at her.

"Your reputation infers he's wrong about you. He is wrong, isn't he?"

Offended, Jen swallows her pride. "I haven't begun. I see what I'm up against. Your file is understated. No matter."

Gordon smiles, walking away. "I'll get the Coke Zeroes."

Jen calls after him. "No, make mine a regular Coke with lemon from McDonald's."

Gordon turns back to her. "Very cool. You saw the delivery."

Jen smiles. "That was my part of the order. You'll have to get his Zero from the storage locker."

Gordon disappears. Jen leans against the wall, her thoughts running to her last assignment. Breaking Amir Ahmad Zaire was nothing compared to this Irish-American. A total "Fubar."

CHAPTER TWO

Search and Sniff

Carefully Jen watches the aging guard, Pete, free one handcuff so Wolf can grip the drink. It is the hand Wolf asked to use, his left. Wolf shocks Jen once again by simply chugging the entire Zero Coke. His eyes water, but he doesn't cough or gasp from the carbonation. His toothy grin reveals the slightly yellow teeth of one from the Midwest, perhaps Iowa or Nebraska. She had noted his mention of the town Chadron. He offers no resistance when Pete fastens the free hand into the cuff. She muses to herself that she was correct in assuming he was left-handed. Or was he deliberately trying to fool her? No question, this dude has her off center.

Pete exits.

Jen sips her McDonald's Coke, pauses, then asks, "Why are these so much better than Cokes from a can?"

Wolf blinks. "That's your question? I could answer but it's rhetorical. Interrogation setups won't work on me, Jen. Been through too many. Why not just leave? Let some fuck start the water boarding."

Jen sighs, putting down her Coke. "We don't do that anymore. You've been there, done that, you know the drill now."

Wolf stares into her eyes. "How long before you ask when, where, and how we plan to hit?" She remains silent.

"You can't pick up network and cell phone chatter on these hits."

Jen's eyes widen at that unintentional clue. Or was it intentional?

He continues. "You're due to be blindsided. I'd bite my tongue off before helping you." His smirk is huge.

"We'll see," Jen mutters as she sips the Coke again. She mentally files away 'these' hits.

Just a hint of irritation is in his response. "Not even if you fucked me."

She grins. "No chance."

No smirk as he mocks her. "We'll see." Silence. He looks away then quickly back at her. "Wait, of course!" A genuine smile now. "You're a lesbian."

Her eyes narrow on him. "Do you really think so?" She wins this one. He gently shakes his head, purses his lips, and carefully says, "No." He almost yawns. "But you dress like Rachel Maddow."

Jen nods. "Yes, and she is very smart."

His voice is not without contempt. "Like you."

She opens the file again. "We'll see." She removes the cap from a black Precise V5 Extra Fine Pilot pen and checks something in the file. Finally she looks up at him.

"Your father lives in Texas."

Wolf snaps promptly, "I was born in San Francisco. Migrated to west Nebraska. I'm just a cowboy. You know, like Biff Loman."

Jen stares at him, deciding to pretend she does not know the reference. "Your father is Republican. A fan of dumb Governor Perry, no doubt."

Wolf glares at her and takes the bait though recognizing it as such. His mind is seething over mention of his father. He is determined to get her off the subject. "Perry dumb? No. You mistake a lack of sophistication for dimness. I can't abide the man but don't underestimate him. He might be one who learns from mistakes. How about you?"

Now into it, Jen engages. "Perry has only mastered the appearance of doing something. You should try thinking in terms of Realpolitik. See things as they are not as you wish them to be."

"Ahh," Wolf sighs in pleasure. "You're one of those women we used to call dames. You read Cormac McCarthy at bedtime to learn about mankind's inherited darkness. Shit, have you even been to Iraq let alone Afghanistan? Did you just fly in and right out of Baghdad and the Green Zone certain you knew the land and its folks? Northern Iraq is awash with blood, blood clots, drying blood. Loose Jesus-lover heads are used for soccer by ISIS fighters. Your so-called leader dithers, dithers, dithers. The French dither too, even after their comic book publishers drown in the blood of free press calamity. Meantime, we lop off heads and burn evil Jordanian pilots in cages a la Joan of Arc. You think the U.S. military is viable in Iraq by posting National Guard troops on the border. At least Governor Perry can say, 'I could see Mexico from my house, could see the coming of criminals and I did something about it!'"

Jen's mind is whirling—stop him and whip him at his own game or let him exhaust his venom? "You done?"

Wolf snarls, "Not until I finish off Texas and your insipid question about my father—dead to me in that state! Perry has better credentials than the woman the Democrats worship, you know, the one with Benghazi around her neck like recycles from a landfill of cheap, bogus pearls. And frequent-flyer John Kerry looks like a man who sees presidential timber in his mirror. He even looks okay while being admonished by Netanyahu, 'Don't ever question me again!' I say the same to you, 'CODE' Jen!"

Jen resorts to a comfortable and earned laugh. "Wolf, now that you've reestablished your well documented hatred of America and its leaders, I confess I find your exoneration of the Texas Governor bogus. You're no conservative let alone Republican."

Wolf snaps back, "Really? Then who am I?"

Jen finally squares off as she stands and leans her palms on the table to create a strong position of dominance.

"You are a defamed former junior college professor of English Composition and Philosophy who came to view the biochemical process of life as meaningless, OF COURSE! Wolf, be you West, East, South or North, meaning IS possible! If you and your mindless, butchering ISIS buddies would be capable of thought, you'd realize that if some absolute plan, purpose, whatever, actually existed, then no particular action would have meaning except as a single element in that total—rather like the movement of a single mote in a ray of sunlight, or a bit of dust under your bed. Since there is nothing absolute, what you and your kind do today could be meaningful. However, not if you behead innocent people or burn them alive in a cage. You must have enjoyed killing the young American girl and passing it off as a Jordanian air strike. The reason you and they are NOT going to win is because you refuse to allow the emergence of human consciousness, which introduces awareness and the possibility of reflecting on your own actions. Rather than rage and scourge, try actually thinking. Meaning is possible but only if you put down your rifles, knives, gasoline and matches!"

Wolf whistles and sits back. "My. My, my. Sweetheart, I didn't understand a thing you said, but I was galvanized by your effort. No, I was no professor of philosophy, were you?"

Jen sits, not spent, but pleased. "No. There are few, if any, philosophers due to cultural decline. The paucity is owing to fear of where questions may lead. Questions can cause convictions to be abandoned. Yes, I'm after answers from you. I'll get them. We can exchange questions if you wish, but memory and imagination will enter into our answers like a code we each will have to decipher. You and I are in a condition of time. We know that you know when some hideous attacks will occur. We know you know where and how. You think your task is to divert and confuse me. My task is the same. In this room alone, we sense that this is all there is. We're too curious to remain silent. We've already proven that fact. Questions will be asked, all kinds. Slowly, convictions will be abandoned. When even wrong or misleading answers start to proliferate, the persistent questions will drown. One of us WILL win. You will tell me what I want to know. You may not even know you've told me, but you will."

Wolf takes in a deep breath and says with simplicity, "Jasus H. Christ, you are full of yourself."

Jen smiles. "Takes one to know one."

Calmly, Wolf asks, "What do you want to know?"

Jen laughs. "Very good, very good. I'll use your trick and answer your question with a question. What do you want to tell me?"

Wolf spreads his long fingers wide toward her like a plea. "Take these off. Bring me a Starbucks cinnamon dolce latte, extra hot. Let's talk."

Rising and heading out, Jen turns back to him at the door. "The cuffs remain... for now."

That smirk again. "Leaving me so soon? Heavy date? Rush to childcare? There can't be a husband. Partner? Need a Scotch? Vodka?"

Jen says over her shoulder, exiting, "That's six questions. Slow down."

Wolf is laughing as the metal door slams. Jen smiles as she walks to the elevator.

Starting her '66 classic white Ford Mustang with a black leather top in the Bureau parking garage, Jen snaps in the special seat belt she had installed, and heads toward Foggy Bottom. The April air is brisk with the smell of spring rain. *The Nationals might get their opening in after all.*

Dusk is falling as she turns on to New Hampshire Avenue and into the driveway of Notti Bianche, stopping at the side entrance of the restaurant. She flips the keys to the valet. "About ninety minutes, Raul." He nods. She stops in the small bar, picking up the Grey Goose and tonic with lime prepared by Silvia when she heard the Mustang arrive.

Walking down the long hall, Jen stops to see if Dan already has a table. He does, far in the quiet corner they prefer. Dan Cauble cannot see her, but he hears her footsteps and rises. His old lab, Smokey, jumps up too. Jen pets Smokey first, hugs Dan, and sits with a sigh. As she takes a large swallow of her drink, Dan says, "Can you talk about him?"

Startled, Jen replies, "How did you know?"

Dan smiles. "I can smell him. Pungent."

CHAPTER THREE

Love and Loss

Jen automatically sniffs her jacket sleeve. Dan is right. A faint but distinct acrid odor wafts into her nostrils.

"I'll insist they shower him before the next session."

She considers how acutely the other senses operate when one is blind. Dan rarely discusses what happened to his convoy in Afghanistan, but Jen was relieved that the handsome veteran suffered no other injuries in the explosion. He now works as a valued counselor for the V.A. His work with wounded warriors is outstanding, earning him a fine reputation and salary to match.

Dan's injury, along with his remarkable continued service to the country, has served to cement her desire to do her job in extraordinary fashion. Ten years as a successful field agent has earned her the plumb spot in D.C. as the top interrogator. Chief Gordon was the new one not her. Jen smiles at Dan and asks, "Have you ordered?"

Dan nods. "Yes, steak with fries and the broccoli rapini. I told Luigi to order your butternut squash soup with mushroom risotto as soon as you arrived. Oh, I added the antipasto salad with house dressing as a side. Okay?"

"Lovely," Jen replies, finishing her drink. Smokey begins to snore beneath Dan's chair. They laugh, Dan noting that his gentle guide is aging.

After the meal and espresso, Jen kisses Dan lightly and sees him out the front door with Smokey. Fortunately Dan has a nice studio apartment just down the street on New Hampshire toward Watergate and the Kennedy Center. Smokey knows the route safely, perfectly. As Jen observes Dan open a small umbrella to the peppering rainfall, she ponders for a moment about Dan's proposal to marry. She quickly dismisses the thought, anxious to get back to her place to prepare some very specific questions for Wolf.

She knows she cannot simply continue in highly arresting verbal debates. Hard, fast specifics will be next. Later she will try more covert methods. He is as formidable as any terrorist she's met. She thought Al Qaeda had been tough, but this ISIS American tops the list.

The drive across Key Bridge into Georgetown and her little apartment near the university takes only ten minutes. Parking the Mustang in her slot, she heads for the elevator to her third floor. A dark-skinned man with long black tresses under a beret watches her from the stairwell. Sensitive and alert as always, Jen glances that direction, catching sight of him. He immediately turns and ascends the stairs.

Inside the elevator Jen pauses. Her training nerves kick in. She pushes the button for the fourth floor. Once there, she goes to the stairwell, peering down. Silence. Nothing. Carefully but quickly she descends to her third floor, Mace in hand. She unhooks the holster strap on the Ruger 380 with a crimson trace laser under her jacket. Empty hall. She enters her apartment calmly but efficiently, looking over her shoulder.

Inside, she pours a small glass of dry sherry before sitting in the coved window seat and looking out at the rain. Street lights glimmer with a crystal shine. Suddenly a man dashes from below her across the street disappearing into the darkness.

Sleep is restless. In her dreams she is on her grandfather's farm in Iowa trying to sell the beloved house to women wearing burkas and niqabs. She wakes with a start at four a.m. Jen pops a Folgers gourmet hazelnut cream cup into her Keurig, heats it, and stares out the window. Rain is still falling.

Wolf awaits her, showered.

CHAPTER FOUR

History and Hiding

Jen arrives in the Interrogation Room before Wolf. She glances at her Timex— 9:00 a.m. It is Friday the 11th. The Nationals were, in fact, rained out of their opening.

Pete ushers Wolf into the room locking him into the cuffs. Wolf is freshly attired in a clean, orange jump suit, his hair still damp from the shower. Jen thinks Gordon must have been hit with a sniff ordering the shower and fresh clothing. She smiles.

Wolf tilts his head. "Why the smile? Glad to see me?" Jen nods. "Absolutely. Freshly presented too."

Wolf smirks. "Yes, I complained that I could only be with you after a shower and fresh duds. By Christ, they obliged. You must have status, honey."

Jen opens the file intent on ending chitchat. She snaps out a comment.

"You knew Basaaly Moalin, the Somali-born U.S. citizen in San Diego."

Wolf quickly responds, "Did I?"

Jen continues. "Moalin was found guilty of sending large amounts of money to the Shabaab, an extremist Somali militia with ties to Al Qaeda. Explain that to me, Wolf. You graduated from Al Qaeda to ISIS?"

Wolf repeats, "Did I?"

Jen realizes this is going nowhere. "Okay, let's go back further in time. Your career really began when you met Nawafal-Hazmi and Khalidal-Mihdhar. They were taking flying lessons in San Diego and so were you. This was 2000 right?"

Wolf sits back and sneers. "I was in San Diego once. Took in the zoo and the water park. Felt sorry for the Orcas."

Jen persists. "You lived with these Arabs in the godka."

Surprised, Wolf now responds. "You know a little jargon. Of course you do. No, the Somali word for 'cave' is not appropriate. I lived in the old Winona Garden district, Jen, the Bandar Salaam Apartments. All sorts of people, all kinds of nationalities. Very American, a melting pot, baby."

Progress was going to be rough, but he had admitted to San Diego and the key location there. She continues. "Were you not a key Hawalas agent, handling money transfers for Islamic groups?"

Wolf reverts to form. "Was I?"

Jen tries again. "We have a photo of you with the notorious Aden Hashi Ayro. You and this Somali guerrilla were close, clearly. Did he tell you about his renowned meeting with Osama bin Laden prior to the 9/11 attacks?"

Wolf snaps at her, "Ayro is dead."

Jen smiles. "Not when this photo was taken, sir."

He replies, "Photos can be easily falsified, you know that, honey."

Frustrated that direct questioning is getting nowhere, Jen makes one more attempt. "We have another photo of you with Issa Doreh, a college-educated man like you. We know that he helped a charity that gave indigent Somalis a traditional Muslim burial. The photo shows you and he engaged in fadhi ku dirir, literally 'sitting and fighting.' These no-holds-barred bull sessions led to lovely events such as 9/11. You have quite a history for a lad from San Francisco's exclusive Hill district!"

Wolf starts to reply but catches himself. Making it clear the specific questioning is pointless, he relaxes and spews words as though writing a lame-versed poem.

"Sugar Tits, darling Jen, I know nothing about Somalia or such people. The photos are no doubt manufactured by your digital labs. I have been to Russia, however. Ah, sweet illusions, like imagining Ukraine as a nation removed from Russia. Nostalgia for Kiev, Crimea, and Odessa. Your government does nothing while your President is lost in a haze of confusion and Capitalism. Now, moving on to Iraq. It's true that your Republicans allowed the rich to plunder your economic resources. Iraq ought to have been conquered, not saved from itself. Democracy is not going to work for all peoples. In fact, it works for none. You sound like another academic liberal making no attempt to comprehend the world beyond constructing a wish list. The world's people cannot just 'get along.' All cultures are not equal. You're filled up in America. Out of room. The world's out of room."

Jen snaps, "Bullshit."

Wolf motors on. "Planet Earth ran out of human carrying capacity by the mid-1970s. You liberals won't admit that this President, a kind enough soul it seems, is incapacitated by his character just as Woodrow Wilson was after his stroke. In America's world of baseball, a prick like Leo Durocher was right when he ridiculed 'nice guy' Bill Terry. Americans have sons who, for all their talents, cannot and will not function. No warriors, no winners. Spoiled by riches and entitlement. Boys drowning in swimming pools with warm chocolate milk, drowning and insisting on whipped cream as they fail to swim. You left the field of battle to the Sunnis and the Taliban."

Jen jumps to her feet. "ENOUGH! Cool off and shut up. Then I may be back to talk, not listen to madness!"

Wolf laughs richly as Jen leaves, smarting in momentary defeat.

Outside, Jen walks briskly to the window where Gordon stands staring in at Wolf who babbles on relentlessly to the window, knowing they are there.

"You were warned about allowing the formation of Israel and the displacement of the Palestinians. No one listened to the Middle East specialists of old, the Christer-do-gooders who founded American University in Beirut and served in your State Department through World War II. That history was pertinent. You have Israel, a sovereign nation, a special-relationship friend of sorts. As for the Arabs, the House of Islam divides and subdivides. The Palestinians have no friends. They are tools. Long gone the 1993 handshake between Rabin and Arafat at the White House. The world is not perfect. Bad-ass Hebrews are easily hammering the perpetually foul and fouled Palestinians, the fucking morons of the theocratic Islamic persuasion, the Hamas/Muslim Brotherhood. It's a bad ugly slaughter. It's like watching a great heavyweight fight a tomato can. And Putin's faux Ukraine cadres placed land mines around the wreckage of that Malaysian plane. Imagine a fresh corpse, strapped to a loose seat, falling thirty thousand feet through the roof of your barn or chicken coop or guest cottage! Shitteroo land mines around a crime scene keeps detectives at bay. Pass the vodka. More Pelmeni, easy on the salt in the pork broth!"

Jen jumps in. "Slow down, Wolf."

He ignores her. "More Kalishnakov's! Putin lives alone, really, though a former Olympic gymnast is having his latest baby. Putin does not like to smile. A smile gives too much too easily. More vodka. Please pass the borscht. Chocolates from Belgium. Putin has wild bears helicoptered in for private hunts. Then he helps with the gutting, skinning, butchering. Steaks all around. 'Ukraine is not a nation!' Putin phones your President, 'Shove your sanctions up your ass.'"

Wolf ends with a hearty laugh, sighs, sits back, and closes his eyes. Gordon and Jen stare at one another.

CHAPTER FIVE

El Jefe and El Jen

Gordon nods to follow him and heads up the hall, Jen trailing him like a squaw, resenting it. He makes it worse by opening his door and entering ahead of her.

Jen dejectedly follows Chief Inspector Gordon into his office. She deliberately shuts the door with a crisp bang. They sit. He looks at her, silent. Finally Gordon speaks.

"You never had a chance. I thought you were making progress when he slipped that there was more than one strike planned. Except for that, you lost ground today. You allowed him to dominate. You lost control at the end."

Jen fights back. "A battle, not the war. Besides, I learned something else."

Gordon flashes his own kind of smirk. "Really? What might that be?"

Jen meets his gaze squarely. "His verbal tirades reveal a man given to education, history, baseball, and theatrics. They reveal a mastermind at work, probably frustrated that he has no lemmings listening in a classroom. He's no doubt a frustrated writer or maybe a ballplayer. And he's an actor. I hear a man given to games and puzzles. A Stephen Sondheim writing political lyrics. He may be given over to ISIS slaughtering but he's better suited to being in Congress if he dropped his obscenities."

Gordon relaxes, smiling. "Very good. That's more like it. So, what's your plan, what next?"

Jen smacks her lips, thinking. "He dodged all the specific references I offered from known associates in the past. I think we were wrong picking him up so soon in Nevada. We thought he had gone rogue, a lone wolf. My guess is that he was on his way to Las Vegas where there'd be more cover. I think he would have met compatriots there."

Gordon asks, "Who?"

Jen replies, "No idea which ones, but likely those who would carry out the actual strikes."

Gordon nods. "Are you thinking whatever the plans are, he's the mastermind? He reports to no one and has his own cell?"

Jen nods her head. "Just a hunch, but I think he's frustrated by the minds he once took orders from in Iraq and Yemen, let alone the Taliban in Afghanistan. I also think his being west was a diversion after his days in San Diego. My gut instinct says the hits will be in the east."

Worried, Gordon goes on. "New York? D.C.?"

"One or both, Chief. I now think it will be here."

Puzzled, Gordon asks, "Why?"

Jen replies, "I'm certain I was followed home after dinner with Dan last night. Someone was in the parking garage at my building. He darted away. He hung around a bit because I caught glimpse of him again later from my window. Wolf has compatriots here. They're very likely operatives who will carry out his plans."

Gordon objects. "We trailed him a week in Reno. He saw no one. We snatched him up before he used his ticket to Vegas. No one knew we had him."

Jen smiles. "Come on, Chief. When he failed to show in Vegas, they'd put two and two together."

Gordon continues, "But they wouldn't know if we were

CIA, FBI, or private contractors. How would they know it was us? We brought him here in a private jet. How would they latch onto you? And why?"

Jen's reply is low-keyed and gentle. "Chief, you warned all interrogators to always figure on a leak."

Gordon frowns. "Only two knew, both agents in Reno, the plane crew, you and I. Are you suggesting a traitor?"

Jen shakes her head. "No, no, though anything's possible. Just a casual slip of the tongue by any one of us, any time, any place. They're no less resourceful than we, just as we were taught. If we can use a drone to both see and listen at hundreds of feet, if we can spook cameras and microphones into almost any location, so can they."

Gordon protests, "Not down here. Not down here where we are now."

Jen nods. "I agree. I think it's different down here, but there was a degree of vulnerability getting him here."

"Well then..." Gordon speaks as he rises, "Any 'games and puzzles' you may try with Wolf better be good."

"Yes, they better be."

Gordon puts on a light trench coat. "And you better not get hyper in the combat and blow it. I know you have a remarkable gift at spotting small clues and adding them up. The problem is, how long do we have? Your way takes time."

Jen rises too. "I'll press but it won't be in one session. He'll never break. We'll have to piece it together. When you can't be at the window, take the recordings with you. Whatever his plan, it had to be a long time in the making. My guess is that 'operative plants' were set up and established long in advance. With the right clues, we can check on personnel in likely target areas. We can then intervene and disrupt."

Gordon nods, frowning. "You'll need luck, not just skills."

Jen laughs. "That's always the case. Every strike we've

prevented since 9/11 was as much luck as talent. We also missed. Boston."

Gordon sighs. "How large are his targets is what concerns me most."

Jen almost laughs. "No doubt as large as his ego. I expect he will divert, strike with contained limits, then go where it's considered impossible." She pauses, blinks. "Possibly the other way around. Think of a boxer. Left hook usually follows with a right cross."

Gordon nods. "Or an uppercut."

Jen closes the imagery. "Fatal body punch to the heart."

"Precisely," Gordon says. "Caution, Jen. The Seahawks just lost the Super Bowl by an aggressive, imaginative coach's bad call."

Jens smiles and nods. "And the dour, frowning coach kept to detailed defense and intercepted on the bad call."

"Yes," Gordon concludes. "You need to be both those coaches rolled into one. You need great luck not just good luck."

They exit together, speaking not a single word on the slow ascent in the old elevator.

Hummingbirds return to Jen's mind. She realizes she needs to put fresh, sweet liquid in the feeder outside her small kitchen window on the third floor. Energy. She will need energy to plan the next foray with Wolf. At her parking slot in Georgetown, Jen looks around carefully before exiting the Mustang. No one. Nothing.

As she disappears into the elevator, the dark stranger in the beret steps out of the shadows and walks to the Mustang. He looks around slowly before leaning down near the rear of the vehicle to attach a small piece of metal under the frame next to the slender silver exhaust pipe.

CHAPTER SIX

Transcending and Tricks

Prior to entering the Interrogation Room, Jen stops to study Wolf through the window. He looks calm and clean, including a shave, which makes his silver-streaked mustache seem bright and trim. His eyes are closed. Jen ponders, smiling to herself. Perhaps he uses torpor. No question he's into some sort of meditation. Does he use a mantra?

The thick metal door shuts beside Jen as she sits across from Wolf. His eyes remain shut.

After a few moments Jens speaks quietly. "I've had my mantra for years."

His eyes do not open, but Wolf replies just as softly, "Join me."

Silence. She figures this is the start of the game for the day. She closes her eyes. After a moment she realizes that she should be doing this in earnest. She repeats in her mind, "Karingg, Karingg, Karingg..."

Suddenly Wolf speaks, eyes wide open. "Enough. I don't want you elevating and flying when I can't unless this is the day the cuffs come off and we talk with parity."

Jen blinks her eyes open, properly. "I never elevated or flew, but I could probably manage it now that I'm older."

"How old are you, Jen, thirty-three?" He smiles with no sign of the smirk.

Jen is ready. "Thirty-three will do indeed. And you are, oh, forty-eight?"

Wolf sits up very straight. "If correct, a differential of fifteen. We both look younger than our years, don't you think?"

Jen shakes her head. "I think you look exactly forty-eight and I feel like seventy-eight."

Genuinely surprised, Wolf cocks his head. "Do you really?"

Jen responds quickly. "Yes. My work takes its toll. Women age faster than men, don't you agree?"

Wolf does not respond. Now he is suspicious. He shifts gears to a familiar tactic, words, but he remains with the subject at hand.

"Probably, but most women are merely unhappy due to a self-inflicted lack of achievement which they instinctively feel may be cause for sympathy. Being at peace with a lack of achievement is an offense that cannot and will not be borne even by the people who love these women the most. It becomes any woman to fight like a Tamburlaine against all odds. Persevere, dear Jen, find a way past your inability to cope with me, let alone break me."

Jen retorts smartly, "You remind me of a possessed conductor overwhelmed by Beethoven's 'Seventh Symphony.' You're a desperate man drunk with the heroism of your own 'music.' You're merely relentless like the continuation of a long and undying past. It's you who can't cope with me, let alone break me."

Enjoying a true adversary, Wolf leans forward. "Speaking of the 'Seventh Symphony,' do you know the story of how Elia Kazan and Arthur Miller used it to inspire the actor, Lee J. Cobb, to find the spine of the role of Willy Loman during a tryout of *Death of a Salesman* in Philadelphia?"

Stunned, Jen pauses only for a breath. "I get it. I refer to Stephen Sondheim and you feel the need to respond in kind. Okay, tell me, Wolf, how did the 'Seventh' serve them or did it?"

Wolf races on. "Salesman was opening at the Locust Street Theater and Cobb was floundering without the requisite tragic size needed for his role as Willy. Across the street from the theater, the Philadelphia Orchestra was playing Beethoven's 'Seventh Symphony.' Kazan and Miller dragged Cobb to the symphony hall and sat either side of Cobb in a box, inviting him to drink in the heroism of the music. That night, Cobb flung himself into the role without holding back! Jen, you're the one behaving like a possessed conductor of the 'Seventh Symphony.' However, that may be natural because you're a woman aging, which always leads to retraction of self. It's a primary impulse."

Jen doesn't skip a beat. "No, you're aging, a terrorist without a country. You remind me of an ancient Chinese Emperor trying to write verse and sing songs in a secluded garden. Look around, Wolf. This is no garden."

Right on cue, Wolf snaps. "I prefer a Roman Emperor for the fable, Jen, say Caesar Augustus, ensconced on an island of pretty boys and girls. Retirement into seclusion can be either rich and productive, or it can be an ingrown toenail of the soul. Sorry, Jen, I am far from retirement."

Jen fairly leaps on that assertion. "How soon would you like to retire, Wolf, it's April. By summer?"

Wolf starts to respond but stops. He leans back. "You're so eager for any clue. I'll grant you one, free of charge. I won't retire 'til late in the year, or maybe next year." The smirk is huge.

"I don't believe you of course." Jen leans back and deliberately closes her eyes.

Wolf turns reflective, knowing he is in tune with her. "I should hope not. We could strike America tomorrow. And the next day."

Silence as Jen latches onto the 'and' rather than 'or.' The plurality slips could not be calculated; he's too instinctive when engaged in exchanges. She's convinced there will be two strikes against the country. In the silence, both relax, eyes closed again. Was he honest about late in the year plus next year, or deliberately giving her misinformation. Her frustration grows. She returns to her mantra to get control.

In the momentary silence, she reflects on his known education, his brief teaching at a junior college in Oregon. He was English composition, remedial labs, one introductory philosophy course, part-time baseball coach. Far removed from music and theater, yet he refers to them. And speaks like a self-appointed historian/philosopher. Why?

Wolf opens his eyes, returning to the subject of women and aging. No question, she's struck some chord. His voice is calmer.

"I knew a girl, not unlike you, only Irish. Hair like Maureen O'Hara."

Jen considers. *Now he adds film to his cultural mix. He likes to talk, that's a fact. He seems to like talking to me.*

Wolf continues wistfully, almost lyrically.

"The lass and I walked Ireland together. She would be forty-three now. In my dreams, she remains twenty. However, a woman is a gatekeeper. She would have tamed me. Had I married her, she would wake up now and ask, 'What am I doing in bed with grandpa?'"

Jen tries to stay with him. "Ah, erotic promiscuity."

Wolf chuckles, a chortle. "No, promiscuity is indiscriminate, casual, from Latin 'mixed up.' Actually, promiscuity can be educating, a great source of confidence, a spur to work. However, I was not mixed up, I was never promiscuous. I might be with you, not the Irish lass. Sex is just fun and shouldn't lead to anything or away from anything, except reassurance about acceptance and approval."

"Are you philosopher or artist, Wolf," Jen asks seriously. That provokes a different tone and response.

"Plato I am not. That asshole argued that artists, meaning, artisans, the Greek is 'techne'—those skilled with technique—artists don't know how they do what they do. They're unreliable witnesses to their own work. I found teaching was like that and abandoned the profession. Terrorism is far more engaging."

"More bullshit," Jen replies. "Something happened to you so staggering you left all your considerable learning, sports and yes artistry, behind you. Whatever it was, it had to be very powerful for such a crazed transformation into primitive behavior."

"Well, Jen...," Wolf replies, leaning as close toward her as the cuffs will allow, "no woman motivated the transformation. No man can stop us. No woman."

Jen matches his stare. "Bruce Chatwin would respond to that arrogance with an epigraph: 'Lovers are the only ones who get into the mystery.'"

On that note Jen rises quickly and heads for the door. Wolf stops her with a question. "Christ, you've read Chatwin! Wow, are we lovers?"

Jen does not turn around but says carefully, "Of course. The killing kind. Try not to dream tonight."

Outside the door she leans back and forces air out a few times releasing tension. Today was a terrible risk, but she leaves confident of gain. She reflects, *if this were baseball, I stand firmly on first base.*

However, when she stops at the window for a last glimpse at Wolf, he is waiting. He growls a hack and expectorates all the way to the window, a liquid cloud smearing, dripping, canceling his image. She turns away, nearly gagging. She enters the elevator, almost trembling.

CHAPTER SEVEN

Dark Eyes and Dim Eyes

As the white Mustang exits the Hoover parking garage, Jen looks left as she turns on to Pennsylvania, not noticing the dark blue Rav IV to her right.

In it, Ahmed Mubark and Rahm Shuja are following the magnetic signal hidden below Jen's vehicle. Faisal Saleh is at the wheel if they lose the signal and have to move. This is their final test run.

The signal works perfectly, blinking red when Jen turns off the ignition in her apartment parking slot.

Ahmed is ten years older than Rahm. They are old friends, educated in Dearborn, Michigan, then Lansing. They met after joining a local partisan group. A year of conditioning and training was followed by jobs in D.C. in 2005. In 2012, both succeeded in moving from original placements to a larger site. Ahmed is a skilled sous chef in the kitchen and Rahm a heating/cooling engineer's assistant in the basement of the popular Fogo de Chao restaurant. The trendy establishment features the finest arrays of meats in the city, prepared with an Argentinian array of delicious spices.

Both men descend from families in Yemen. They are skilled in both English and Arabic languages. Unmarried, the two men dedicate their lives to the cause of "anti-American imperialism and military murder," a popular phrase dating back to a radical leader in their Michigan mosque.

As the older of the two men, Rahm was the first of the duo to be approached by a persistent customer to the restaurant, Ashram Saade, a wealthy landowner and real estate attorney from Arlington, Virginia.

Ashram was granted access to the kitchen to congratulate the chef and staff. He slipped his card to Rahm who followed up contact the next day.

What Rahm and Ahmed learned was a guarded secret. Two fellow travelers from Yemen had been strategically placed in two famous D.C. establishments shortly before 9/11. Each man had impeccable credentials, happily married with families, educated at George Washington University and Howard University, respectively.

Pasha Qureshi was another well-trained and skilled heating and cooling system junior engineer. Abdul Wissa had nearly identical credentials. After thirteen years of dedicated, flawless service, the two men now carry approved, unquestioned job clearance and contracts for employment in the two grand facilities. Unlike Ahmed, Rahm and Faisal, both Pasha and Abdul married, each with two children, sons to Pasha and daughters to Abdul. The children are all in middle school in D.C., both wives proper homemakers. Neither family has any idea that the paternal head is ISIS, though all are devout in their religion. Pasha and Abdul both memorized the Koran when mere teenagers.

Both men have easy access to all vital machinery in the bowels of two of the more important locations in the city. There is no reason for further vetting. They are checked annually but routinely. No one in the hiring chain has any idea that the men have been secretly, discreetly conditioned over a decade by a radical Islamic loving

American leader, the conditioning managed totally by electronic communication.

Pasha, Abdul, Rahm, Ahmed, and Faisal constitute a quartet. They are the most dangerous cell operative in the United States. Their leader is "Wolf West" who became the liaison to their financier, Ashram Saade. In the west for some final fun, Wolf was unexpectedly picked up at the airport in Reno.

These patient terrorists know that the gains achieved over years of stable employment service by the cell are about to climax in two of the largest, deadliest strikes against America in history. There is one remaining obstacle. Their ISIS-American leader, "Wolf West," is currently imprisoned in D.C. A superb inside operative plus expert surveillance have them keyed on his female FBI Interrogator, "Code Jen." Somehow the terrorists have to free Wolf, the man who has put everything in place for "Operation Duplex." The secret inside operative sees Code Jen as a threat to their plan. He informed the quartet about this woman. However, her appointment as Chief Interrogator came from high-placed directives. The inside operative knows that once she is out of the way, he can dare to provide a path of liberation for Wolf who can lead the attacks. The quartet needs Wolf's funding channel and final leadership to implement the deadly strikes. The inside operative will be out of the country before then. Chaos and destruction will follow, leading in time to a "new Islamic nation." Such grandiose ideals have ravaged Earth from its beginnings, seemingly culminating in what Hitler and Stalin attempted.

Jen again sleeps in fits and starts. The dream is an old "Time Marches On" newsreel of those two twentieth-century megalomaniacal monsters. The dream turns to nightmare when memory of Wolf's laughter breaks into the silent newsreels, awakening her.

Jen's head is throbbing. She pads into her bathroom,

takes two blue Aleve tablets, then sits on the stool, trying to focus her mind after the nightmarish slumber. Something is bothering her beyond the challenge of the interrogation. Her mind races. *What is it? What is it?*

A hot shower and shampoo help. She blow dries her hair as she studies her face in the sweating mirror. Lines in her forehead are deepening. A slight squint reminds her of the appointment in a week for the annual eye checkup. Noticing the squint a few days ago, Gordon told her to add some sort of eye supplement. A call to Dr. Liz Stang led to the purchase of PreserVision. Taking two a day was no big deal, but she dislikes any kind of pill popping. However, there is something cool about the dark rose, smooth little pills. They remind her of the red room in "Downton Abbey." She muses as she swallows one, upper class, all the way. She prides herself that at age thirty-three she's never smoked, not even marijuana. Total absorption in career is her daily "high." Sex had been of quickly passing interest after losing her virginity as a college freshman at Drake University in Des Moines. He was a pre-law student with a minor in economics. The allure faded fast with her first course in criminal justice.

There was no one special until she met Dan and fell in love for the first and last time. She knows this as well as she knows anything. If only real passion accompanied the love. However, she often reminds herself, you can't have everything. She laughs at the idea. "Fake it 'til you make it."

Rather than begin the day with the usual caffeine, she puts a Bigelow Breakfast Tea minus the buzz in the Keurig. She adds a shot of half and half plus a packet of Sweet Leaf. Sipping the hot, smooth liquid in her favorite, if chipped, Redskins cup, she ruminates about the politically incorrect team name. The cup is also adorned with a tiny drawing of a black beret honoring the manufacturer of the cup, "Beret Vessels."

She knows! The dark man with the beret in the garage. It is not "what" is bothering her, it is "who."

Jen finishes the tea. She speaks aloud to herself, as she often does. *Has to be connected.*

Jen notes the bright sun, opting for a light jacket over the usual dark pantsuit. It's not that she doesn't wish to be relatively attractive as a woman, it's simply that it doesn't mean a thing to her one way or the other.

"Part of my confidence," she once answered a question about it from her beloved mother, gone four years now from COPD and Waldenstrom blood cancer. Jen misses her upon waking as though her passing had been the day before. An only child, she certainly loved her father, but a heart attack had taken him nearly fifteen years ago. She kisses that Mason ring every morning, kisses her mother's portrait as well. Her mother is smiling by green bushes near the Eiffel Tower in Paris. Jen never fails to remember that lovely trip they had together.

Almost out the door Jen has what starts as a lark from her discovery. She probes the top shelf of the hall closet, locating a cloth brown beret. Placing it sharply on her head, she smiles in the mirror and winks. The smile fades. Why am I doing this? she whispers. She tosses the beret on the shelf and leaves, making certain the special lock sounds behind her.

In the garage she looks around slowly just in case. It's only 7:00 a.m., not a soul in sight. However, she walks slowly around the Mustang.

Nothing seems out of order.

As she drives toward the Bureau, she glances high on the windshield where a sticker announces her next vehicle service: 4/20/15.

Satisfied for the moment, she whips into a McDonald's drive-in lane for the daily large Coke with lemon. One buck. What a deal. This is going to be a good day.

Not far away, the Rav IV pulls to a stop. The green light

on the metal locator has turned red. Ahmed lights a small, dark cigarette. He makes a notation on a clipboard and drives toward Fogo de Chao. He loves food preparation. This is going to be a good day.

CHAPTER EIGHT

Faiths and Fools

Wolf is sitting with eyes closed as Jen enters. Assuming he is in his form of meditation, Jen sits with her Coke and a paper cup. He opens his eyes and speaks.

"Where's my Zero?"

Jens smiles and says, "On order. I brought an empty cup if you'd like to share."

Wolf eyes her carefully. "Can I trust you?"

Jen shrugs her shoulders. "I'll drink first from the straw. You'll be safe."

Wolf nods. "Just a bit, two fingers."

She pours accordingly and he nods, drinks, then adds, "This stuff is deadly. And you'll gain weight."

Jen responds, "I work it off. It's an addiction."

"Like our love, eh?" Wolf strikes her as hungry for communication.

She responds from Shakespeare, a small test. "This love will undo us all."

Engaged eagerly, Wolf snaps, "Troilus or Cressida?"

Taken aback, Jen is silent.

Wolf whirls on. "You don't know. That's okay, Sugar Tits, after all, trying the Bard on me is behaving like a balderdash 'wee hoor.' You tend to shift tone like a histrionic high school girl, shaping your malaise with every error. Every full Professor of English in this country should be required to wear a goddamned Trojan condom over his or her head... for life."

Jen counters. "I think you taught Shakespeare once upon a time."

The smirk. "I did? Maybe, maybe not. I will tell you this since you don't know. 'This love will undue us all' is neither Troilus or Cressida, though it's from that play. Helen says it, darling, Helen. Think about her. She was right."

Jens responds, "The one Shakespeare course you taught must have stuck with you."

Wolf smiles. "I just have a mind for trivia, a good thing to have. Your file says I was English composition and philosophy."

Jen tries a different approach. "The King of Jordan may fly sorties himself in response to the pagan executions your brethren are pulling off for video propaganda."

Wolf cannot resist responding, "King Abdullah is not his old man, nor is he his grandfather, Faisel, who rode alongside Thomas Edward Lawrence. King Abdullah is a product of Western Civilization. *Star Trek*. Jasus Syphilitic Christ, he'll fly the jets we gave to Jordan. Hopeless. You can't bomb ISIS away. Your government is fleeced by the Jordanians. The king visits your top man, you pay his airfare, hotel room, fill him with grub, booze and bullshit, then send him home to fly sorties. Jordan is a place for the criminally insane. The king whines over a lost pilot. Like the Palm Beach bartender who complained to Dr. Hunter S. Thompson during the Pete and Roxanne divorce trial, a dog had taken his place! Hunker down, King and President Dither, the worst is yet to come. That goes for you, too, 'Code' Jen, hunker down."

Silence. Jen's mind is whirring. How in hell to engage this speechmaker keeps eluding her. She latches onto an idea.

"Wolf, perhaps I should water board you after all."

That does give him pause, but he smirks. "Sure, as long as you do it instead of some muscle-bound hairy ape."

"Ah, you can handle water boarding no doubt."

"I paid my dues. You should try it."

Her reply is incisive and surprises him. "Oh, in my training at the Presidio in San Francisco, my unit had to go through it. It's a terrifying experience. We had a set of numbers to repeat if we wanted it to stop before it was officially ended. I never used the numbers. The technique goes back to Genghis Khan. Only we who remained silent passed."

Wolf genuinely admires this and nods. "I'm impressed, seriously."

Jen adds sweetly, "I'm also a Tae Kwon Do black belt. File that away if I ever remove the cuffs."

Wolf leaps on that idea. "I'll risk it. Come on, honey, get out the key."

Jen merely laughs lightly and opens the file. As she does so, Wolf clips a menacing question at her, "Are you Jewish?"

Surprised, Jen looks up at him. "I know a little Jewish history."

Puzzled, Wolf pursues this. "Prove it and I'll decide."

Jen hesitates, but looking for a path in this maze, responds, "Since the Babylonian Talmud of 486 B.C. through the Spanish Responsa, 13th to 15th Centuries, right through Spinoza and Martin Buber, Jews have tried to come to grips with the significance of turning the Life Blood of Egypt, its Nile River, into real blood, as stated in the break away from Egyptian slavery. The meaning is deep and complicated."

Wolf is fascinated, sits back, and listens. Jen goes on, tables turned.

"One of the most important characters in the story of

Exodus is Aaron, brother of Moses. He spoke for Moses. Why? The Talmud says that Pharaoh was advised there would be an attempt to overthrow him. All eyes fell on child Moses. So Pharaoh brought a metal replica of his crown, had it heated to a white-hot temperature, placed it in front of child Moses, who reached out and touched it. Immediately Moses put his hand to his mouth and burned his tongue. From then on, he spoke with a stutter. Moses needed Aaron to speak for him when he went before Ramses. The importance of this is significant to Jews—their lives always depend on brothers. Now, in this story, Joshua is absolutely necessary because it is he who wants to fight Pharaoh, not Moses. The moving part of the story takes place after the Red Sea drowns the Egyptian army. In Heaven, God is crying while the angels are yelling for joy. Michael asks God why he is not joyous for the salvation of the Hebrews. God replies, "How can you laugh with joy when so many of my Egyptian children have died this day."

Wolf sits up. "With my hands free, I'd applaud. Not for the well-known story, but for your effort to see if you can find a point of humanity in me. Sorry, Jen. We're not all God's children and we don't all have brothers. However, yes, I think you are Jewish."

Jen leans forward with satisfaction, holding up her right hand. On the middle finger is her attractive ring with a large diamond in its crown, which points upward like a stalagmite. "That was my father's ring, Wolfey. He was a Mason. I was born and baptized a Christian. However, my personal faith is none of your business."

Wolf whistles softly. "The Mason ring itself is prosaic but that blue diamond cost your papa over ten grand. Ever cut yourself with that thing?"

Jen smiles. "I'm very careful and I take it off at night. Jewish be damned. Chalk this up as my day."

Jen rises to leave but Wolf speaks as she reaches the door. "Wait. I think you need help. If you're willing to talk to me seriously about your darkness within, I'll reciprocate. This love affair needs a foundation based on personal insights and exchanges. We can leave politics, war, and mayhem aside. Hell, I'll even sing for you, if you wish. Remember *The King and I*? 'Getting to know you, getting to know all about you... getting to like you, getting to hope you like me, getting to know you, that's...'" He breaks and says quietly, "What do you say, Jen? Want me to go first?"

Slowly, inner satisfaction suppressed, Jen returns to sit. She pours a little Coke into his cup. She sips on the straw, leans back, and says, "Age before beauty."

CHAPTER NINE

Within and Without

Wolf chugs the Coke she gave him and announces, "Wolf's Darkness Within." He reverts to disinterested monotone.

"Nanny after nanny, best private schools in the city. Played baseball. College then short stint in pros. Durham. Actually caught Bob Feller in a bullpen session. English major, Philosophy minor. Worthless. Father had abandoned spoiled mother and her inheritance, drifted to Texas. Never saw him again, good riddance. No sibs. Teaching a wasteland. Bad system, self-serving faculty, selfishly greedy administrators, one student in a hundred worth mentoring. The government increasingly corrupted by military, industry, Wall Street, incompetent Congress and leaders. Bush/Cheney and Neo-Coms destroyed what remained of the American Dream. Master Dither lost in reflection, contemplation, negotiation, and the 17th hole in Georgia. With ISIS we have a simple goal. Kill as many as possible, including Muslim pacifists, then, far sooner than later, take over this continent. Establish an ISIS nation with our version of Islamic faith and order. From here, control the world until it blows up. And it will."

Wolf sits back and adds, "How about something to smoke? Anything will serve."

Jen snaps, "No smoking."

Wolf responds, "Chaw? Copenhagen?"

Jen smiles. "In your Bull Durham dreams."

Wolf perks up. "You know a little 'bout the game?"

Jen nods. "My father played some, big Dodger fan." Silence. She is taking a note.

Finally Wolf asks, "Your Darkness Within?"

Playing along, Jen sighs, also resorting to a monotone.

"Iowa farm, standard schools. Drake. Ended up in pre-law. Dated a low-level agent, chose the Bureau. Accepted. Toughest field training. Placed in Interrogation. I like it."

Wolf is agitated. "We both left out anything personal."

Jen tilts her hair, the ponytail sliding. "The Game was Darkness Within, not Lightness. Your file has no mention of marriage or family."

Wolf laughs. "Someone with a cracked skull and swollen brain must have compiled that thing. Burn it. I had a wife and four kids once. You have no factual record on ol' Wolf at all beyond that one teaching gig and my approximate age."

Jen dives in. "Oh, we know of the wife and four kids. Under different names, right? And we know what happened to them. Before that, we know you lived in Nebraska where you were a faux cowboy, Biff Loman indeed."

Wolf snaps at her, "Now who's bullshitting?"

Jen continues. "Your wife and kids loved you but paid the consequences for your bad decisions. You finally refused to remain on a parenting matrix. You took up with a damaged girl who helped you destroy everything good in your life. Then she disappeared. After you floundered in contemplations of suicide, you drifted to San Diego. We've already covered that scene. This is your last chance to save yourself, Wolf, save the man you were and lost. Simply tell me who is helping you and what the plan is for massive madness."

Wolf stares at her, but his mind is racing in awe of what

she seems to know about him. How did she determine that solitude and time turned him to ISIS? Did she really know what happened to his family?

His mind flashes to the two-lane highway south of Colorado Springs, the old farmer asleep in his Ram swerving head on at them.

Impossible, Wolf thought to himself. Different names then... yet...

Jen went on speaking. "Stop holding yourself hostage and give yourself to me. Only I can help you now."

Wolf continues to stare. Jen muses to herself. *At least he's ceased the verbal assault. I hit some core in the man.*

She adds aloud, "You're too gifted with words and ideas to relish the slaughterhouse of ISIS and remain there. Do you know the writer, William Melmoth? I bet you do. Think about this: to believe that life has no value is to lament the loss of that which we always possess and cannot discard or lose, and is just as rational as to die of thirst with a cup of water in our hands."

Wolf struggles for parity, a balance, some level of control. Finally, he exhales and responds. "The only way I could give myself to you would be in bed. Or, remove the cuffs, and on this table. Perhaps you like it standing up. Honey, your insights are guesses, they come and go so fast they can hardly be called real. The past and future do exist, at least to the matter of experience we are currently limited to. Energy leaves an imprint on the 'fabric' of all that is extant. Somewhere, sometime, everything we ever did or will do continues to happen in its own quantum capsule. Well, Sugar Tits, an altered state, be it alcohol, drugs or ideology that creates it, is all that matters. You think you know what crippled me, don't you? You think what crippled me was placing almost the entire sense of my own self worth and human value in the perceptions of a wonderful wife and exquisite four children. My wife was frightened and lonely most of the time. The end of that is unknown to you or anyone." Now he lies. "Even to me."

Jen senses immediately that he is trying to obfuscate the truth. She fires back at him. "More bullshit, Wolf, you can't escape into one of your winter night of words! Be straight with me. Talk to me! We can make it all matter again!"

Wolf reaches back for all he's worth. "Good fucking grief, woman, what matters about bad hiring, botched jobs, tomato cans, Vaseline tubes, used pissy-mops, downer pills? The country is overrun with punch-drunk, gay, Jewish theater folks, millionaire athletes and actors, media pundits, and politicians. Only your military can save you now and to do it they must kill every fucking last one of us. Shit, we're only about forty-thousand ISIS. Drop one or two atomic bombs and its over. Don't worry about the collateral damage. Hiroshima and Nagasaki prompted no concerns. Let it fly, it's your only chance, Toots!"

Jen can only fight on. Sensing she made genuine headway, she has no recourse but to let him rage and listen to him carefully. She snaps. "You LET IT FLY, You FUCKER! Not what is wrong with US! What in hell is wrong with you?"

Wolf never misses a beat. "What's wrong with me IS what's wrong with you and this fucked-up country! America's bedrock is NOT guns and slavery, as most of your blathering network and cable pundits scream. The rock you were founded on, yes, the rock I was founded on as well, was used-up, crowded, English and European population. Later add Africa and Asia. The Irish Famine sent two million people to North America, hundreds of thousands over to England and to Australia. Those hounded Irish were starved down to eating grass. Then religious kooks from England, the starved of Ireland, plus gold seekers from France and Spain sailed to this land. Look around now. Racism and other pathologies as much in black communities as anywhere. Where went all that socio-babble about 'Post Racial Society,' the very gibberish we heard in 2008 when The Dither Master swept into office on a wave of dimwitted sentimentality and wishful thinking."

Jen breaks in, "Enough! Shut up!"

Wolf roars on. "Nobody can stand that creature from Alaska, but I grimly chuckle when she asks, 'How's that hopey-changey thing going for you?' Samuel Beckett was right that the academic world bulges with anus grit. Look at the degrees of so-called higher education in the outdated halls of ivy from Harvard and Yale to Stanford and U.C.L.A. 'Doctors of Education.' What? A Ph.D. in Composition Theory? What? An M.F.A. in Musicology. What? Theorists on writing who cannot, have not, and will not ever write a sentence their mommies would find memorable without the careful use of tracing paper. Your Master Dither will retire, withdraw into golf and teaching at a university which, to some measure, makes its dollar with anus grit and online degrees. You scream about our use of torture? A hideous, grotesque departure into evil? You call us Terrorists. Well, the theo-crazies were combatants in the service of your adversaries. Some fought for the Taliban regime and that institution had nation and state legitimacy."

He pauses. He has her rapt attention.

"You and your guy, Gordon, take the night off and go to a symphony. A play, make it a stupid musical. Better yet, go watch the Nationals with their pitching staff of bloated salaries. Jasus Syphilitic Christ, give myself to you?"

He chuckles, closes his eyes, relaxes.

Exhausted, Jen rises, taking the two empty cups with her. Neither says a word. Before the door closes, she cannot resist looking back at him. He sticks his tongue out at her as the clang of the door rings in her ears.

CHAPTER TEN

Friend and Foe

Chief Gordon is waiting for her when she turns the corner to head down the aisle past the viewing window. He motions to follow him, which she does. She glances at Wolf but his eyes are closed in seeming contentment. Following Gordon to his office is a minor offense to Jen; she feels like a squaw again subjugated to the rear of a warrior. At the door, Gordon makes it worse by entering first, leaving her to follow and close the door, which she does just a trifle loudly. Gordon looks up at her and snaps a question. "Where do you plan to take the personal stuff?"

Jen replies quietly, "To some point of personal connection."

Gordon raises an eyebrow suspiciously. "To what end, trust?" He doesn't wait for a response. "You know damn well he can never be trusted and he's too bright to trust you."

Jen sighs. "I'm not so sure. I'm in there with him. You're behind a window."

Gordon snaps, "So?"

Jen sits up a bit. "I can see his eyes, hear his breath, watch for sweat or mannerisms."

Gordon relaxes. "I see. Your psychology work with the

CIA coming to bear."

Jen smiles. "If you wish. Look, Chief, I'm compiling both clues and trained guesses."

Gordon asks,"Tell me about them."

Jen hesitates, then wonders to herself why she did so. She becomes instinctively cautious. "It's early, but I'm taken by his sense of history, sports—and his theatricality."

Gordon nods. "Listening to the two of you is impressive, I must say. Two highly charged intellects with loads of information."

Jen responds at once. "That may be true, but what's important is more visceral than cerebral. I have to either please him or agitate him to the point of a revelation worth pursuing."

Gordon leans back. "None thus far?"

Jen returns the question. "Have you picked up on any?"

Gordon leans back, eyes closed for a moment. "Just his utter contempt."

Jen nods. "Yes, that's paramount. His contempt for the government, our education, us above all. Contempt feeds him. I need to get him past that somehow."

Gordon frowns. "Through the personal stuff?" He adds with just a touch of sarcasm. "The darkness within?"

Jen nods. "Possibly. It's worth a shot. Direct questioning from our vetting went nowhere."

Gordon purses his lips. "Most vicious contempt I've ever heard from a prisoner."

Jen's eyes widen. "I agree. There was a phrase once from one of the men he referenced, Arthur Miller. Miller once referred to 'a sewer of contempt.'"

Silence as Gordon ruminates. Finally he concurs. "Perfect, no question. Wolf swims in a sewer of contempt."

Jen nods. "Questioning him at times is like paddling a canoe with a tennis racket... another image from Miller."

Gordon chuckles and asks, "And why do you match up

with Wolf and this writer?"

Jen shakes her head. "Wish I knew. Then I might really learn something."

Gordon persists. "No, I mean you seem as conversant with Miller and his work as does Wolf, maybe more so."

Jen retreats. "Got me. I took a Modern Drama course at Drake. O'Neill, Miller and Williams remained with me."

Gordon dismisses the subject. "Not me, never liked plays. Movies are much better."

Jen asks, "Really, why?"

Gordon shrugs. "More real to me. Funny, I s'pose, but an actor on screen is more believable to me than alive on stage in front of me."

Gordon rises to get a cigarette from his jacket flung over the back of a chair by the old-fashioned hot plate holding a ceramic coffee pot.

"Jen, be careful with the personal stuff. And never let him out of those cuffs. You tease him that there's a chance."

Jen rises, noting that Gordon is lighting a Turkish cigarette, a Murad.

The aroma is familiar to her because Amir Ahmed Zaire chain smoked them till she called a halt to it. She seizes the moment to ask a question.

"That reminds me. Why are you allowing Pete to move him from his cell to Interrogation alone? Isn't that risky? Pete's no kid."

Gordon exhales as he answers, loving that cigarette. "Pete's only alone from the elevator to the I-room, just a few feet. Officer George is always in the elevator with them. Pete's a senior officer, the only African-American in the unit who speaks several languages. Besides, without an accomplice, Wolf has no place to go down here. The stairs are behind solid steel, the elevator has multiple guards at the top and George who rides down with Pete and prisoner."

Jen lets the matter drop and opens the door. "Anything else?"

Gordon takes a big drag on the Murad then exhales. "We're counting on you. ISIS needs a boost against our bombing. Recruitment's crucial for them. They need to hit us along the lines of 9/11, especially since Congress voted to make the conflict official."

Jen acknowledges with a simple, "Yes, sir." Some instinct propels her to ask, "Oh, Chief, may I ask where you get the Murad smokes? Dan loves expensive Turkish tobacco but can't find the best."

For an instant Gordon pauses. Then he casually responds, "Sure. Georgetown Tobacco Shop, M Street. The only place in the city that imports S. Anargyros tobacco. Where did Dan pick up the habit?"

Jen smiles. "Afghanistan, where else? How about you?"

Gordon narrows his gaze on her. "Had a tour in Istanbul. Nasty habit but no one mixes tobacco like the Turks."

Jen acts deeply interested. "Really? How so?"

Gordon decides to overwhelm her as though unfairly challenged.

"Yaka for richness, Serres for mildness, Mahalia for coolness, Zekni for mellowness and Bafra for aroma. Goes back to 1892, Jen. Try one with Dan."

Jen shakes her head. "Impressive, Pat, you know your tobacco. I'd never try one. Not after choking on Murad smoke from Zaire." She turns to exit but he stops her.

"Zaire was allowed to smoke in Interrogation?"

Jen turns back to him. "I tried it as a means to get him to relax. It worked, but I couldn't take it."

Gordon smiles and waves the cigarette. "Now I know. Pardon me, Jen, never again in front of you."

Jen laughs lightly. "No sweat, sir, I'm not interrogating you."

Gordon levels his gaze at her. "I wasn't sure."

They both laugh. She leaves, closing the door carefully behind her.

She pauses to breathe and think a moment. Not at all certain why she is filing the past ten minutes away in her mental folder, she nonetheless does so, including the observation that Gordon was somewhat defensive about Pete. He took the Murad question nicely in stride. She walks briskly down the hall, stopping at the window to watch Pete unlock Wolf's table cuffs.

Jen is startled that he unlocks both hands rather than one at a time. Wolf just stands there while Pete places new cuffs on him for transport to his cell. Jen is even more startled to see Wolf lean toward Pete, his back to the window. He must have said something because Pete nods before placing Wolf in front of him. They exit the room as Jen rounds the corner. Pete looks surprised, but is polite when he speaks to her.

"Officer George will be down to get the man to his cell with me. Sorry to make you wait, but no one allowed in the elevator with us."

Jen quickly responds, "Of course, Pete. I'll take the stairs."

She turns and walks away. Wolf says loudly enough for her to hear, "Pete, that is a really choice derriere. Do you envy me?" If Pete replied, Jen did not hear it.

Jeb finds the other coded card for the steel door to the stairs. As she enters, she muses to herself about Wolf's reference to her rear. Well, one connection is secure.

At that moment, she hears the awful laugh from the sewer of contempt.

CHAPTER ELEVEN

Hearth and Heart

Dan and Smokey are waiting in her apartment, both in the small but elegant modern kitchen. Jen can smell pasta and sauce. Accustomed to not looking up, Dan greets her happily, "Hey, babe." Smokey waddles to her for a hug. Jen then hugs Dan, kissing him lightly on the lips. He pulls her back for a real kiss. This always startles her.

Jens drops her jacket off her left shoulder and arm, unsnaps the holster and weapon, slips them off, placing them on the counter. The jacket is pulled back on fully. She goes to the bottle of Apothic Red wine from a Modesto vineyard sitting in a small, wooden carrier.

As she pours two glasses, Jen says, "Not a special or expensive wine, why do I like this stuff so much?"

Stirring the penne, Dan replies, "Perhaps because we toured the vineyard together. Our first romantic weekend."

Jen sips rather than respond and Dan adds, "Where have all the flowers gone?"

Jen sighs, too tired to deal again with the fact that she never really found sex to be a main, let alone casual, connection between them. She loves his humor, at least before Afghanistan, and adores his intellect and support. He's as handsome and sexy as a man can be. Even without sight he loves to take care of her, which she both likes and dislikes. Once again she feels selfish, knowing all too well why she keeps delaying marriage.

Finally Dan asks, "Hand me the colander, hon, time to strain this penne."

Jen puts down her wine to take over the task. "Here, let me. Don't want you burning yourself again."

Dan picks up a family Jewel Tea leaf bowl noting, "I made the sauce from scratch. Mama's favorite recipe."

Jen adds warmly, "And her favorite bowl. Not a chip on it."

After a quiet meal, Dan asks, "Never seen you this preoccupied, even with Zaire. Anything you can tell me?"

Jen sighs and replies, "Wish I could, I really do. It's not just this prisoner."

Dan persists. "What do you mean?"

Jen relaxes a bit and tries to answer. "Well, the way, the method, how he's been handled seems to me... I don't know. Unusual or special, something."

"Dare I ask how? Can you give me an example?" Dan needs to know, wants to know, worried about this unique woman he loves so unconditionally.

Jen pauses then answers, "Not really, but I wish I knew Chief Gordon better. I've been with the Bureau longer. He seems old school when it comes to women."

Dan reacts. "Did he say something, do something in that way?"

Jen protests, "No, he never said anything off center. He seems, well, guarded somehow. He has no common social courtesy."

"Toward you?" Dan asks.

"Yes...," Jen responds reluctantly. "Nothing overt, just subtle things like opening a door for me, a kind of superior attitude or tone to his voice."

Dan chuckles. "I get it, but you're a very sensitive person, maybe too sensitive, hey, babe? He is your boss, after all."

With a touch of temper in her reply, Jen says, "I have never minded authority as long it was courteous in manifestations!"

"Hey, don't flare at me, I'm on your side. Anything else?"

Jen pauses. "Someone else, our senior officer in charge of prisoners. He seems a bit casual with security."

Dan nods. "That does sound odd, certainly risky. What does he do?"

Jen demurs. "I can't divulge more. I've already said too much. Just an uneasiness both above and below me in the ranks. Also, this guy, this prisoner, Daniel, he's like from another planet."

Dan smiles. "Really? How so? Pointed ears, laser eyes, what?"

Jen shakes her head. "No, no, no, I'm serious. Dan, this man has an extraordinary mind. I mean, exceptional, unique. He's like Winston Churchill and Hannibal Lecter rolled into one man."

"Good God, Jen. Does he want to eat with you a glass of chianti and a side of fava beans?"

"That should be funny, love, but it's not." Jen finishes her wine. "He's that rare creature of the highest and lowest specimen. He can be amusing, articulate, adroit as hell and suddenly profane, crude, coarsely erotic. He's both appealing and scary."

Dan pauses before responding. "How do you think he perceives you?"

Taken aback, Jen asks, "What do you mean?

"I mean, does he find you much the same, both appealing and scary?"

Jen pauses before answering. "I suppose so."

Dan nods. "Right. Isn't that your job? Match up and then win?"

Jen replies simply, "Yes."

Dan goes on. "It's a stalemate so far?"

It is not easy for her to say it. "Yes."

Silence.

Dan risks one more question. "In all honesty, is he more appealing than scary?"

Stopped cold, Jen hesitates.

Dan continues. "Since you don't know, I understand your preoccupation. You don't know how to continue."

Jen retorts, "Oh, I know how to continue."

Dan quickly adds, "But should you?" Silence.

She says softly, "I don't know."

Dan sighs. "Nonetheless, you know you will continue on whatever path this is going?"

Jen is quick to say, "I have no choice."

Dan flares a bit himself. "Yes, you do."

Jen ends the exchange. "No, I do not." Silence.

Smokey pads to the door and emits a familiar whine. Dan rises. "Smokey needs a break. So do I."

Nothing is said as Dan slips on a jacket and Nats cap. He puts on the leash, hating those handle things. They depart, leaving Jen alone at the table.

She rises and clears the dishes into the dishwasher, putting the remainder of the pasta in the old Jewel Tea leaf bowl with aluminum foil over it

She puts on her jacket as her blue Apple iPhone 5 tingles. She answers, "Yes? What? When? I'll be right there."

She scrolls the contact list on the phone to Dan and rings him.

"Hey, sorry about that. You at the park? I was going to join you but I have to go... no, I'll explain later. You sleeping over? I see. Well, I'll call you later. Be careful... yes, I will. Love you."

She pops the phone off, slides it into an inside pocket, and turns to go. She stops, removes the jacket, puts the holster and weapon over her left shoulder, snaps it firm.

Puts the jacket on again. Stops at the Apothic bottle, holds it up to the light. About an inch remains in the dark black vessel. She chugs it directly from the bottle, hurries out the door, the special lock clicking behind her.

As she wheels onto the street in Georgetown, a sharp flash of lightning rifles through the dark sky above. Jen steps on the accelerator, shooting many yards before the pervasive clap of thunder seems to shake the vintage Ford. Her mind flashes on Mustang horses running from a pursuing truck in northern Nevada. She speeds through a yellow light without figuring out where the image had come from.

Only when Jen wheels into the Hoover parking garage does it come clear to her that Clark Gable and Marilyn Monroe were in that truck behind the frightened Mustangs running for their lives. She blinks as she hurries out of the car thinking, *What the fuck, Arthur Miller again*!

CHAPTER TWELVE

Tears and Tales

Jen finds Gordon waiting for her by the Interrogation window. He frowns and snaps, "Take a look at this."

Wolf is sitting quietly, weeping.

Dumbfounded, Jen mutters, "What the fuck—"

Gordon nods. "He raised a scene in his cell, insisting he be brought down here to see you. I thought he might be ready to talk."

Jen continues to stare. Gordon adds, "Pete and George brought him down. He was quiet 'til Pete cuffed him. He just started sobbing."

Instinctively, still muttering, Jen says, "It's an act. He's a goddamn actor."

"Okay," Gordon responds. "Why this? Why this sobbing? Shit, real tears. He's a mess."

Jen pulls her code card out of her jacket pocket. "Must be 'Method' trained."

Not understanding, Gordon asks, "What? Method what?" However, the door has swung open. Jen enters, stops, the door slams behind her.

Wolf's head is down, tears still flowing. Gordon goes to the window as Jen sits in her chair and waits. Suddenly, very suddenly, Wolf stops weeping. His head comes up, eyes open. The smirk.

Jen is too wise to speak or ask anything. Finally Wolf relaxes and starts rattling.

"Here's the thing about what's happened to education. It's what's wrecking this country faster than we can do it in ISIS. Check out Dostoyevsky. He had insights into this even as a Russian. Whoever has experienced the power, the complete ability to humiliate another human being with the most extreme humiliations, willy-nilly loses power over his own sensations. The only educator in this country smart enough to write about this is a fellow named John Holt. Tyranny is a habit, it has a capacity for development, it develops fully into a disease. The habit can dull and coarsen the very best people to the level of a beast. Blood and power are intoxicating... the person and his or her citizen dies within the tyrant forever. To return to human dignity, to repent, to rejuvenate, becomes almost impossible. This mess began with the parents today who don't give a rat's ass about their children's education. The teachers are soon reduced to babysitters. Bullies begin to humiliate the weaker who are usually the brighter and loved by caring parents. Corruption runs rampant. The American ideal of free and mandatory education is dead. Teachers are obligated to be tyrants. Administrators are worse!"

Finally Jen leans forward and almost shouts, "Enough! Stop it!"

Wolf leans back and smirks again. "Darling, I was providing a valuable lesson about the futility of this country's foundations. I didn't get to finish."

Jen fires a question. "What in hell's with the morose, fake sobbing? Actors' Studio tricks to get me down here at night?"

Wolf shakes his head. "I'm wounded to the quick. You didn't believe me? Sugar Tits, I missed you. Couldn't sleep. Need to see you and explain more about my life and disillusionment. We agreed to look at the Dark Within together, baby!"

Jen smirks right back at him. "I'm onto you, Wolfey. Did you use 'Affective Memory' or the 'Magic If' for that Oscar?"

Wolf laughs. "Whoa! Now look who's spouting Lee Strasberg nonsense out of Stanislavsky bullshit!"

Momentary silence, then they both break out into long laughter. Dismayed outside the window, Gordon lights a Murad and inhales deeply.

Jen finally speaks. "What did we just do?"

Wolf grins, not a smirk. "You're supposed to be the brain here, Madam Interrogator. You tell me."

Jen turns serious. "You've had training, experience in theater."

Wolf shakes his head. "No way."

Jen counters, "Film? You don't reference Strasberg and Stanislavsky from idle reading."

"Again, you underestimate me, love. I'm very eclectic. One should know something about everything and a lot about one thing."

Jen persists. "How to accomplish mass slaughter of innocents."

Wolf retorts, "Just who is innocent?"

Jen reverts to the beginning. "Regardless of the method, you got me down here. Don't ever try that again."

"I won't have to because you're finding the same need to be with me as I find with you."

Jen shakes her head. "No, drop that tact right now. I only need to see you to stop you and your mindless comrades."

Wolf pauses a moment. "What makes you think I have comrades? I'm the lone Wolf."

Jen smiles. "Says you AND your file—mostly misinformation."

Wolf is intrigued. "Really? How many comrades do I

have?"

Jen's verve picks up. "At least one is watching me, perhaps two or three. They're not the key players. Probably a few more, less than four or five. I'd guess a quartet cell."

Wolf cackles to hide his admiration. "Desperate guessing games now. Oh, Jen, you can do better than that, come on."

"I'm leaving. This will cost you tomorrow. No Coke Zero."

"Wait!" Wolf urges. "At least let me finish my screed." Jens sits back down, saying nothing. Wolf resumes.

"The tyranny that schools and school people exercise over the young is milder than the tyranny about which Dostoyevsky was speaking. Schools don't have the power of life and death over children. But they do have the power to cause them mental and physical pain, to frighten and humiliate them. To destroy their future lives. That power has been enough to corrupt deeply the schools and people who run them, teach in them. That power turns those people into petty tyrants. Most of them didn't start out to be tyrants—some may recognize it and regret it, but, too late. Only if the schools in this country rid themselves of the power syndrome can they save their own souls, let alone the souls of the students. So goes the main cancer of your society. Even homeschooling won't save it now."

Jen sighs and says quietly, "Fear the man who feels himself a slave. He'll want to make a slave of you. Obedience is the great multiplier of evil."

Wolf is stunned. "You know John Holt. Wait a minute. You had to be a teacher too."

Jen levels her gaze at him. "If we both know about acting and theater, why can't we both know about education? Sam, 'Wolf,' whatever, whoever, your and my intelligence, learning, education couldn't possibly come from the damaged system you describe! Our accumulation into this moment is very simple—'A mass murderer vs. one who will stop him.' I know you're clinging to some past injury. Your rage comes from a refusal to forgive. Forgive who injured you or even yourself. Wolf, you're afraid to forget."

Wolf turns sullen, close to anger. "What I needed to forget, I forgot. How about you?"

Jen asks, "Who did you lose, Wolf? The wife? Four kids?"

Wolf stares at her. "Good riddance. No loss there."

Jen goes on. "A love? Wolf, to lose someone is also to be free."

Wolf clips his words. "Never. The reputation of the dead lives after them."

Jen persists, "Is it Ayro?"

Wolf's head turns slightly, then he stares at her again silently.

Jen nods. "Aden Hashi Ayro. What happened back in Somali with those guerrillas, eh, Wolf? I bet I have it—you also met Osama bin Laden."

The smirk flashes and remains.

Knowing her instincts are sharp and she's in her best groove, she leans back to ask a question that opens Wolf's eyes wide.

"We both like puzzles and games. Our Sondheim sides. Or Arthur Miller if you prefer. Let's offer a favorite from any category and the other responds in kind."

Wolf says nothing. She continues. "I'll go first. My favorite actor is Tom Hanks. Yours?"

Cautiously, Wolf decides to play. *She does know how to engage me,* he muses to himself, then speaks. "Dustin Hoffman."

She smiles and he adds, "You expected Omar Sharif?"

Jen laughs and proceeds. "Al Green."

Wolf cocks his head, curious. "Led Zeplin."

"Not bad," Jen responds. She pauses, thinking fast as she can but not fully aware of what pops to mind. "Lily Tomlin."

Wolf shakes his head. "David Letterman."

Jen says, "Sting."

Wolf snaps, "Natalie Makrova."

Jen stops. Looks into his eyes. "That doesn't match up."

Wolf's voice is low. "Doesn't it? How about Patricia McBride?"

Sensing something dangerous was happening but having no idea why or what, Jen goes in another direction.

"How about Al Sharpton?"

Wolf snaps, "A tax scofflaw, self-righteous clown."

Jen feels she's on a roll. "Bernhard Goetz?"

Wolf shrugs, replies. "Shoots his subway assailants only to be convicted of a gun crime."

"Maybe that conviction was better than being stomped to death." Jen snaps, "Eric Garner?"

"Resist arrest with heart disease, obesity and asthma? A legitimate takedown tackle, not a choke hold whatsoever. Now you want to make me a racist? Sure, black lives matter. And the homicide rate of black-on-black is appalling. Chicago. Black society has much to tackle from within. Isn't that also your cry to Islam? America is now two decades into Affirmative Action! Jasus Syphilitic Christ, Jen. There's a difference between qualified and qualifiable."

Jen goes to what she senses is the heart of his attack, looking for the signal that could mean "Executive Action." She thinks of herself as an Independent but she liked the President from day one. Wolf's ego is so huge, she senses she is on a viable path.

"Wait a minute, Wolf. We elected a black man President, twice!"

Wolf retorts, "Exactly! Dither, Joe Guffaw, Plastic Hillary, Harvey Holder, Damaged Mormon Reid, all of them, destroyed their own party, washed out its chances in 2016. Your top man race-polarized America. Demonstrations and riots will elect a Republican president, just as the crazy-wild-fun sixties elected Tricky Dick Nixon and Spiro Con Agnew. On the other hand, we and, what was it you call my phantoms—comrades? We may bring the whole thing down before that election!"

Jen snaps, "You better hurry, Wolf, 2016 is less than a year away."

Wolf snaps right back at her. "The election's not 'til fall. We might have another Arab Spring, better yet, winter!"

She notes that his head pulls back for a moment on that remark. She notes it carefully and goes on.

"There was no 'Arab Spring.' That was bullshit propaganda. You Saudi-loving chauvinists may have to deal with a woman president. That should drive you even crazier!"

Wolf laughs. "Cold Pants? Ho, ho, ho. Will she even get the nomination at her age and health? If she does, your people will be tired of her shrill self-justifications. What will be seen is the polyester pantsuit woman who drove her husband toward a hot, plump teenager, as well as the lady who fucked up Benghazi."

Now Wolf is almost in a lather. Jen just keeps making mental notes as he races on. "It's a lot easier for Master Dither and Harvey Holder to criticize cops, using the Justice Department to attack police departments rather than take on the bankers who crashed your economy, let alone take on Big Pharmacy or Big Oil. Shame, shame, shame on Master Dither a cautious, race-craven, abject failure. Not one despot fears him, Vladimir Putin scorns him. How about no response to the chubby basketball-groupie bastard in North Korea? Kim Jong Un's computer geeks/hackers near destroyed SONY! Master Dither should tell that Swiss-educated, brandy-swigging, butter-croissant-gobbling shitwit to start digging a deep, deep, deep fucking hole! Then there's the Persians and nukes. No deal can be made there, woman, none! Someone needs to blow the whole fucking thing apart. That's where I come in, Toots!"

He leans back to rest, grinning, smirking.

Jens says quietly, "Not in here you won't and not without your comrades."

Wolf no longer smirks, replying softly, "Maybe. Like the Lone Ranger, there's a Lone Wolf. He will ride free, and alone!"

Rising, Jen says, "Wolves run in packs."

At the door, she looks back at him. "Unless wounded."

As Jen exits, she adds, "Get some sleep. Store the sobbing act. Tomorrow's another day, Rhett."

Jen was relieved not to find Gordon waiting. As the cranky elevator ascended, she started filing what she felt were key clues she found as much in his eyes as in his words. She began taking notes even before exiting the elevator.

All her best instincts were fired, she was certain of it. Accordingly, she did not go to the parking garage. Let the Mustang sleep here, she thought. Out front she hailed the first cab. On the way home she took lots of notes to sort out before trying to sleep.

Neither she nor the cabbie noticed the Rav IV in an alley as they passed. In the Rav IV, Faisal Saleh had seen Jen get into the cab. He eased out of the alley, following the cab until Code Jen was deposited at her apartment building.

Faisal pulled out his phone and dialed. He spoke English, with clarity and an accent. "She took a cab. She must know. She's alone." He pauses, listening. He replies, looking at his watch. "Two fifteen now, check. Yes. She leaves at eight o'clock. Yes. Ready at seven just in case. Garage. Check. Yes. Both of you? Fine."

He ends the call, placing the phone on the seat beside him. He tilts the seat back to rest until Ahmed and Rahm join him at seven.

Inside the apartment, Jen changes quickly into light pajamas, white with little red polka dots, her favorite slippers with leather toes and heels. She sips orange juice, going over her notes.

She says aloud, *Okay, history, film, theater, politics.* She gets out a map of the city. However, her eyes are heavy. Glancing at the wooden clock on the shelf over the stove, she sees it is nearly three-thirty. She must get some sleep to be fresh for Wolf at nine. She goes to her bedroom, sets the rather old-fashioned "Sharp" alarm clock to 7:00 a.m., pushes her new "My Pillow" under her left ear, and falls asleep in less than a minute.

The little clock is ticking though she does not hear it. She isn't even dreaming.

CHAPTER THIRTEEN

Dares and Doubts

Jen awakens ahead of the alarm at six o'clock. She feels refreshed, relieved that no dreams are recalled. She showers quickly, irritated by soap in the right eye. She notices that the right eye is the one starting to falter a bit.

She forgoes the hair dryer, toweling sufficiently to let the long tresses dry naturally over a Green Mountain decaf and an English muffin with orange marmalade. She never fails to remember that John Fitzgerald Kennedy loved orange marmalade.

Switching to a Folgers Hazelnut in the Keurig, she savors the coffee as she examines her notes.

Jen smiles at her recognitions. One: It could be the stadium where the Nationals play. That would be huge. Two: It could be a university, probably a basketball arena. Three: It could be a large theater, perhaps Ford for the symbolism, or, the Arena. No, not large enough. Kennedy Center?

Maybe. Four: Any government building, provided the President was in it. However, at one time or another, he is in most of them. She sighs in frustration. Despite the clear progress, not nearly enough specificity to probe personnel or known threats. She would have to push Wolf hard today, probably through the personal connection now established. She dreads using the sexual factor, but he's made that paramount in his dialectal exchanges. Then there are the handcuffs. For final confidence, he may have to be free of them. She shudders at the thought. Not yet, not yet. Hopefully, never.

It is a bit past seven thirty now. She puts the dishes in the washer, checks her very light makeup, and adds a touch of light pink lipstick. Ruger and holster secure, she slips on her usual jacket over the blouse. She should have pressed the slacks. The sharp crease has faded and the shoes are not ready for polishing. A glance out the window shows a cloudy day. There is an umbrella in the Mustang, but the car is still at Hoover. She suddenly realizes she must take a taxi. The tiny hummingbird feeder looks dry or almost dry. She notes aloud, *I'll make fresh tonight.*

As she steps out of the elevator in the parking garage, she stops after just two strides. Boldly, the man with the beret is standing at the rear of a car, leaning casually on the back. She is about to reach for her Ruger when Ahmed drops a black hood over her head, tightening a chokehold around her neck in the same action. Jen can only gasp.

Ahmed says in a loud whisper. "Silence. You know the drill. Useless to struggle. Be quiet—follow instructions if you wish to live."

Jen's mind races but she grasps the situation and does not move.

The Rav IV hums to a stop beside them, Faisal at the wheel. Rahm leaps out of the passenger seat up front, opens the rear door, helps Ahmed put Jen in the backseat with him, and jumps back in front. Faisal hits the accelerator hard, speeding out of the garage to the street. He heads into Georgetown.

The chokehold no longer needed, Jen finally gathers her thoughts and speaks. "Wolf will be unhappy. He's expecting me at nine with his Coke Zero."

Ahmed says quietly, "He will see you soon, not at nine."

Jen chooses not to pursue that, but her mind is whirling. She knows she should be doing mental math tracking to gain some sense of the direction they're taking her.

At that moment, the Rav IV slows, stops; the sound of a large metal door is clear.

Ahmed and Rahm help Jen out of the car, placing her on a narrow, metal catwalk. It slants upward as the men lead her up and into some sort of space, Ahmed in front of her, Rahm behind her. She hears a door of some kind open; she is led into another space. Another door opens and she is led into a third space. The men place her on what feels to her like a cot, about her size. There is a soft piece of foam beneath her and a pillow for her head. One man binds both her wrists and ankles while the other slips some sort of mask beneath the hood. He puts the mask over the eyes, removes the hood, and fastens the mask. It feels like a lone ranger mask to her. Not a word is said. Jen resists the strong urge to say something, ask a question.

One of the men carefully yet firmly grips her jaw and gently forces a small, soft object into her mouth. It is moist with cool fresh water. Two solid strings run from the object out either side of her mouth and around her head where it is tied into place securely. Fuck, she realizes. Gagged. That is the worst. She hears them exit, shutting a door behind them.

Jen flashes on a startling thought. Trained for just such an emergency, she realizes she is without fear. Rather, a highly sensitized alertness has taken over all her senses. Breathing is not difficult despite the gag. The mask is better than the hood, allowing full airflow though no vision. Her sense of hearing and smell are magnified. A light aroma of men's cologne had wafted through to her. Not expensive but beats body odor, she thinks. Both men wore tight leather gloves. She had felt the leather.

The man who hooded and choked her in her parking garage had a leather jacket on, smelled new. The first vehicle smelled fresh too. Her current location clearly has air-conditioning. They're well funded, she notes in the file she is creating mentally.

The distinct sound of a large engine is started not far beyond the wall behind her. She sighs. Smart as hell. A moveable cell. Some type of truck or mobile trailer.

The most sobering realization was the comment that she'd "be seeing Wolf." That meant only one thing.

Jen shudders.

CHAPTER FOURTEEN

Exits and Entrances

At 7:00 a.m. in Bureau Headquarters, George is coming on duty when Pete approaches him and speaks.

"Chief Gordon wants Prisoner X moved early to the Interrogation Room."

George wrinkles his brow and replies, "What? Two hours early? Code Jen here?"

Pete heads toward the row of cells, replying, "On her way. Wait by the elevator. I'll get the prisoner."

George is trying to sort this peculiar order out when Pete returns with Wolf handcuffed. The three enter the elevator and descend. When the old lift jerks to a cranky halt, the door opens. Standardly, George steps out to look around. He neither hears or feels the bullet that pierces the back of his skull, tearing away most of his forehead. He drops like cement. Pete and Wolf step around him. They stop while Pete unlocks Wolf's handcuffs. Wolf is looking at George as he speaks calmly.

"Where's Gordon?" Pete points toward the hall where Gordon waits with the door open to the stairs. The two men walk rapidly down the hall. Wolf steps into the stairwell followed by Pete.

It is Pete that now hears or feels nothing as the shot

from Gordon's .38 pistol enters his skull and lodges. Pete stumbles right, grasps the wall, and slides to his death.

Wolf races up the stairs with Gordon close behind. The outside door on the first floor has been blocked slightly open by Gordon who had shut off all alarms. A D.C. taxi, stolen less than an hour earlier, waits. A young Islamic student named Pervez Haqquani is behind the wheel, nervously fingering the roll of money in his hand. As Wolf and Gordon leap into the back seat, Pervez thrusts the roll into his upper front shirt pocket and speeds away.

Not a word is said. Pervez has his directions. He drives straight to The Tobacco Shop on M Street in Georgetown. His passenger leaves the cab quickly, entering the shop with a sign on the door, CLOSED. Pervez speeds away for a mile. He abandons the Ford Fusion, tosses the gloves into a garbage can, then grabs a downtown bus. He is pleased as he presses that roll of bills in his shirt pocket. He will count it again in his room in the dorm at GWU.

In the Tobacco Shop, Gordon never pauses. He grabs the carry-on travel case waiting for him at the back door. Ashram Saade is there, handing him his new passport, a plane ticket to Karachi, Pakistan, and a leather briefcase packed tightly with over one hundred Pakistani Rupees, over a hundred grand in dollars. Much more awaits him in Karachi. After all, he is the highest ranking FBI agent ever to comply and turn for a life time of financial security. He would never see his homeland again, but he is content. Guilt, if any, would come with time. Gordon leaves the rear of the Shop into the town car driven by Hallid Hashemi, another GWU student and able recruit. Pallid has pocketed the same size roll of cash given to Pervez.

Hallid hits the accelerator, heading toward Dulles west of the city. There he will deposit this man he does not know or dare to look at. The trip is made quickly, silently. The Mercury pulls to a stop at Dulles. Gordon disappears into the terminal housing Qatar Airlines. He is in the air by ten o'clock. The FBI alert to all transportation outlets arrives about a half hour later.

When Gordon left the Tobacco Shop, Wolf was busy changing clothes. His own travel and garment bags were waiting for him. He puts on his most comfortable Wrangler jeans, a snap button Ariat shirt, brown, his own, well-worn Tony Lana oxblood boots, and a tan Stetson hat, well used but clean as a whistle. He checks his wallet, swollen with large bills and identifications intact for Samuel T. Worth.

Less than five minutes after Gordon departed, Wolf is out the back door of the Shop and into the night cab of a gigantic Ford Aeromax rig. It pulls a long Wabash trailer built by ten sections, each section three feet long, totaling thirty-three feet in total length, expanded from the standard twenty-eight. The trailer has been designed inside with a ten-foot-long space at front, replete with a cot, a toilet, small sink and shower. A wall with a small door connects the front space to the middle segment.

The middle ten-foot-long segment has a table with handcuffs built into the top with a straightback chair on either side of the table. It is an Interrogation Room! Another wall with a small door connects the middle space to the rear segment.

The rear segment is thirteen feet long with three cots, a toilet, small sink, shower, small stove, and tiny refrigerator from an Arlington, Virginia J.C. Penney store. At the back of the trailer are the standard, large double doors. Beneath the doors is a long metal plank that can be quickly withdrawn to the ground to walk up or down from the rear segment of the long trailer. The entire rig is ventilated, air conditioned, with the three compartments representing the smallest of studio-like apartments. It is a safe house on wheels. The requisite sign on the cab proclaims, "Old Dominion Freight Line, Thomasville, North Carolina." All interstate plates and licenses are appropriately visible and legitimate; though the actual company is unaware that such a rig is on the road bearing their nomenclature.

At the wheel of the truck is reliable Faisal. Comfortably hidden in the back segment of the trailer are Rahm and Ahmed. They are adjusting the up-to-date electronic equipment, replete with a scanner, viewer, radio gear. Small, moveable cameras are outside at various intervals on the truck cabin and trailer. One such camera is in the trailer in the compartment next to the cab. Next to the two busy men is a box with a compact assortment of weapons and small explosives.

As the truck heads into Virginia, Jen is lying on the cot in the front segment or compartment of the trailer, hands and ankles bound. She is relieved that the gag is not large; no feeling she is suffocating. She likes the black sleeping mask far better than the hood.

Aware that she has gone onto a ramp into some sort of vehicle and through two doors into a soundproof space, she can still sense motion. Her acute hearing also recognizes a faint hum from a large motor. The air is temperate and fresh. There is no aroma save the slight remnant of cologne from the men who led her into this space and placed her on the cot.

Jen is confused now about distance and movement, but she thinks she crossed the river and turned left. They must be heading into Virginia. She would try to figure time so she can later gauge how far this vehicle has gone.

She assumes that the three men who grabbed her are aboard. She knows they made one stop before leaving the city. Someone might have joined the trio. She feels a flash of fear as Wolf comes to mind. Impossible, she muses to herself, trying to dismiss the thought. Her mind then goes to Dan. For the first time she feels sick to her stomach. Her next sensation is even more unsettling.

Jen really has to pee.

CHAPTER FIFTEEN

Reverse and Refresh

Faisal pulls the rig into a large truck stop near Royal, Virginia, west of Arlington. He needs coffee. Wolf passes as he calls Ahmed on his cell. Wolf simply offers a command.

"Ahmed, untie her ankles and wrists, remove the mask and gag. She can find the toilet without a map."

Jen is freed, mask and gag last. As she leaps past her captor toward the toilet, she notes he wears a hood, the smell of the cologne still present. He exits as she pulls down her wrinkled pantsuit, nearly ripping the undergarment. As relief cascades over her, she hears the lock click on the small door. Relaxing, she carefully takes in her environment. Neatly done. Portable prison.

Back on the cot, Jen guesses they have been moving from D.C. less than an hour. There was a fairly sharp turn right just past what had to be Arlington. Her first assumption was that they would keep going south, meaning Richmond. If they are heading west in Virginia, she realizes she has no idea what cities are on the route. Would they keep going west?

At that moment, she feels the vehicle move. She tries to concentrate while checking her watch periodically. They had been careless enough to leave the small Timex on her wrist and the Mason ring on a finger. She smiles that she had refused a large, complex watch from the Bureau. She knows the jewelry will be taken when she's dead, maybe sooner.

She looks around to see if by chance they had returned her small case, which she carried rather than a purse. It was gone. It held her identification, Mace, and her phone. When the man had reached carefully inside her jacket to remove the Ruger, he had not even brushed her breasts. She had noted that they were polite to the degree it signaled an Arab to her. Polite but superior.

Jen's training mode kicks into gear. She searches the room for any loose object that she might use or convert to a weapon. Nothing. The only positive discovery is surprising. Only one camera, aimed at the center of the cot and fixed, no motion. She sits on the toilet and looks up; she recognizes the size and curvature of the lens, having installed her share in her field days. Her legs would be in view while on the toilet but, nothing from waist up if she leans back against the tank. She notes that it is worth keeping in mind.

Jen figures it was no longer than fifteen more minutes when the vehicle turned left in a slow arc. She is certain they are now heading south, probably still in Virginia. She reclines back to rest and think as the vehicle whirs steadily on at a moderate speed.

In the cab, Wolf speaks to Faisal. "Route 66 is behind us, 81 should get us to Staunton in about two hours, one hundred fifty-one miles from Arlington. The Sinclair truck stop will be on our right as we hit the city limits. They have a special two-day layover policy. Ahmed and Rahn have to be back at Fogo by day three. The first heat of search and blockade should be over by then. Ashram will let us know for certain. How's the java?"

Faisal shrugs. "Hot."

Wolf leans his head back to rest, eyes closed. His

slight smile emanates from thinking of Jen locked a few feet behind him.

At that precise moment, the Director of the FBI is snapping orders right and left on broad Bureau system communications. He has ordered covers at all airports, train and bus stations, as well as car rental agencies. Main highways have blockades. Photos and basic information of Worth/Wolf are in the air across the country and beyond. Gordon's photo is out there, too, but with no identification beyond, "Also Wanted." The President and Homeland Security have been notified, the country now on high alert. The CIA and Pentagon have been briefed.

The worst job for the Director was calling the families of George and Pete. Teams were sent to each for preliminary investigation. There was no one to call regarding Gordon. A special investigation was already underway on Gordon with the Director well aware his head was on the block with that fateful hiring. Someone had fucked up royally on that vetting, but the buck would stop with him. The Director shook his head, "Must have been a hell of a payoff. He had great credentials."

As news hit the network and cable airways, a call came from Daniel Cauble, well-known military hero and known male associate of Code Jen. Cauble had been unable to reach her, finding her missing at her apartment with the Mustang found later at Hoover. A search of her premises and vehicle turned up an electronic tracking device attached under the rear of the car. Now the Director had the additional baggage of a kidnapped Chief Interrogator. Realizing what was behind all this, some national attack in the planning, the Director was as close to panic as he had ever been in his decades of service to his country.

Not long after noon, the rig pulled into the huge truck parking lot at the Sinclair station at the north limits of Staunton. Faisal found a perfect spot near the rear of the lot to sit for two nights. They would have to head back to D.C. in two days to get Ahmed and Ram back at the restaurant after their short leave.

Wolf went into the station to register the vehicle. Soon Wolf would not be able to step outside. His face and real name will be plastered all over the country on every possible outlet. Faisal crawled into the sleeper at the rear of the cab to rest.

Making certain that no one was watching, Wolf called Ahmed to open one of the large doors enough to allow Wolf to use the metal step unit to elevate to the opening, securing that elevation with the door handle at eye height. Inside, he went to the refrigerator to retrieve a Zero Coke and a large McDonald's Coke with lemon, still holding some ice at the top of it.

Wolf nodded to Rahm and spoke. "Handcuff her to the table, Rahm. Better go along, Ahmed, she might try something. Oh, no need for your hoods now. Let her see your handsome faces. Doesn't matter now."

Somewhat reluctantly, they toss their hoods aside.

As the two men disappear toward the back of the trailer, Wolf checks his face in a small mirror over the sink. He could use a shave but he smiles. Dashing a splash of Aqua Velva on his cheeks and chin, he decides to leave the Stetson on. At that point, Ahmed returns. He has the heavier accent of the two engineers from Fogo de Chao. "She laughed at the table and cuffs. Gave Rahm no resistance."

That news was what Wolf expected from this woman he views as both astute adversary and intriguing female. Rahm enters and nods.

Wolf exits into the middle room with the two drinks in hand. Rahm closes the door and goes to his cot. Ahmed is already resting on his.

Wolf and Jen are alone again in an Interrogation Room, positions menacingly reversed. She sits with long fingers extended on the table. The cuffs are loose enough to allow her to move a bit on the chair. She notes that the chair across from her is padded. Hers is very hard wood. When she sees the drinks in Wolf's hands, she remarks casually.

"At least you added a straw. Is the lemon fresh?"

Wolf is warmly chuckling as he places the drink in front of her. She is genuinely thirsty. With the straw pursed in her lips, she draws a long drink.

When their eyes meet, she has leaned back.

Neither is smiling.

CHAPTER SIXTEEN

Accept and Accelerate

"Like my Stetson, Sugar Tits?" Wolf sips his Zero.

"Gentlemen remove hats in the presence of ladies." Jen smiles weakly. "That includes fancy Stetsons or baseball."

Wolf removes the large hat to the edge of the table and asks, "Cuffs too tight? Do not wish to harm the lady." A hint of menace in that as he smoothes his hair.

Silence.

Finally, Jen says, "You love the irony of this, don't you?" He nods. "Yes, don't you?"

Jen sits up a bit straighter. "I want to know who died."

Wolf glares at her. Freedom always gives him a sense of openness that his tone reveals. "Bare minimum to get it done. Much bigger fish to fry ahead, as you well know."

Jen persists. "How many died? WHO?"

Wolf speaks very softly, but clearly. "Two. The transport guards." Jen winces. "God damn. Pete AND George!"

"No choice, love, no choice."

Silence. She takes a moment to recover, then asks squarely, "Gordon?" The smirk returns as he chugs the rest of the Zero. "Him and his fucking Murad tobacco," she says, hurt but furious.

Wolf exhales dismissively. "Let it go. Long gone forever."

Jen almost snarls a question. "How much did it take to get him?"

Wolf shakes his head in amusement. "More than he deserves or needs."

Jen decides to relax somehow, knowing anger might be followed by fear. She wisely changes the subject. "Three of you. Well spoken Arabs with modest cologne."

Wolf asks out of genuine interest. "How good are you? Tell me, 'Code' Jen, what is our location now? Any idea where we are, love?"

The question intensifies her awareness of the role reversals. She picks up her verve. "West part of Virginia."

Wolf smiles. "Nah, but you impress me with your certainty." In fact, he is dazzled that she knows that much.

Jen smiles. "I'm certain because I'm right. I also know I'm in a big rig converted into compartments. Very accommodating. Safe house on wheels. It can't last long."

Wolf snaps a retort, "It won't need to."

Jen hesitates, then gets to it. "I have no value whatsoever. Why did you bother with me?"

Wolf sighs. "Good question. If we made any mistake, it may have been you. Perhaps I just like talking to you."

Jen senses a small opportunity. "Ah, the Muslim lads are strong and silent, but a tad boring?"

He lowers his eyes at her. "You're in no position to be judgmental, love. Let's put it this way. I've had many interrogators over the years. You struck me as a cut above. I'm curious to honestly learn what you think you know."

Jen meets his gaze. "Just how good am I, is that it? Why would I tell you?"

"Part of our M.O., hon. We like the game. We like being best at it. Let's find out."

Jen cocks her head. "We have time for such games?"

Wolf smiles. "Time enough."

"Then what, Wolf?" Her breath is even. "Regardless, I'm dead."

Wolf smirks. "Are you?"

Jen almost laughs. "Unless your boys fucked up on the route. How can you be sure?"

Wolf is very serious as he says, "You'd be the first to know if they hit us."

Jen nods. "You mean, the first to die." She shakes her head. "Pete and Gordon had no family. George had a sweet wife and two daughters, high school."

Silence.

Jen adds, "You Islamic hypocrites. Savage butchers. You worship death not life. Bastards."

Wolf's voice rises a bit as he snaps, "Enough name calling. To our game. What do you THINK you know?"

Jen hesitates as she contemplates what is to gain by participating, save time. Perhaps that is all she can do. What was it that female Jewish orchestra did in Auschwitz, Jen asks herself. Played for time.

Jen sighs, sips the Coke, and announces, "There are three of you. I believe the cell has two or three more. One of them, someone high and protected, removed, provides funding."

Wolf is mildly impressed but never blinks. "Go on."

Jen reaches back for strength and digs in. "You're all college educated. As the leader, you have the widest experience as well as knowledge. They've been trained to trust you, but, you trust no one. You're the personification of intolerance among the hyper-educated."

That sets Wolf off immediately. She angled well and he bit. He begins quietly but his voice rises as he goes on.

"Such intolerance usually ends with foot-stamping and various quasi-legal procedures. Do I look like a fucking foot-stamper to you? Ask the two transport guards, though I fired neither shot. Your kind of education promotes segregation by race, class, religion. Look at all those bogus 'studies' major. How many au currant 'Queer Studies' Masters programs are there? Who promoted your Dither-in-Chief, eh? Talk about social promotion!"

Jen fights back. "What self-aggrandizing nonsense! ISIS leads to kids who become criminals who become lone wolf killers—like that Hicks madman who killed three Muslims in a rage over parking space while in the middle of a divorce! Such tragedies, like the one you just led at Hoover or the killings by the kid in Copenhagen, such tragedies do not alter the fact of ISIS and how fundamental Islam has metastasized. We should have toppled al Assad four fucking years ago when CNN's Anderson Cooper recommended that the world go for regime change in Syria. Anderson is not anybody's right-wing conservative. He wanted us or western powers to go the subtler route but Putin found that unacceptable."

Wolf laughs. "You make my point for me! No despot fears President Dither. We can help you by bringing him down and the government with him!"

Jen is stunned by that crack and responds, "One at a time or together?"

Wolf growls, "You leap upon misinformation better than actual information. Poor baby."

Jen challenges him. "Okay, tell me, O wise one, how would you take out ISIS if you were in charge?"

Wolf loves this challenge. They are deep in the game again. Time is passing. Wolf feels something akin to sexual heat as he fires back at her.

"We cannot be taken down incrementally. Your bombing only has the pilots and generals looking backward to see how they're perceived. Only a President capable of choosing a ruthless warrior general could lead an army against us and win. Perhaps retired Marine general, James Mattis. And no Brian Williams or Bill O'Reilly along for the ride, real or imagined."

Jen is impressed, deciding to let him rave on, hoping to

gain further clues, not that she will be able to do anything with them.

Wolf is now up, pacing. "A prescription army is worthless. Your military knows that truth. However, a volunteer army is not up to the task either, especially being spread all over the globe. The majority of American sons and daughters are massively sighing, groaning, teeth-gnashing brats calling for equality of service, dispensations, indulgences. A true warrior general with a relatively small force might eliminate us with dispatch, with or without small nuclear arms. A simple hammer and anvil strategy would work. We would have to be hit with rapidity and quick withdrawal. Repeat 'til it's over. Wouldn't take that long. We're yet only forty thousand or so."

Jen interrupts. "You do admire our military, don't you?"

Wolf responds, "Yes! What a shame Patton is not here, eh? You need a warrior-President, too. Teddy or FDR, the 'Buck Stops Here, Harry'! Your best generals ridicule your President. This is not Sparta. You sons and daughters whine about not having chocolate sauce as they drown in whipped cream topped with maraschino cherries. While you wait for me to wield final blows, the world gets quintessentially minor violence good only for stirring folks up because of its proximity. Proximity calibrates insults and hypothetical personal threat. What you don't realize is that ISIS is a phenomenon of a civil war within Islam. You stupidly entered our war. You should have acted with restraint while Sunni and Shi'ia armies and militias, national and extra-sovereign, battle each other unto exhaustion!"

Spent for a moment, Wolf sits as Jen responds. "What a shame you aren't President. You have it all figured out."

Wolf deliberately sips from Jen's straw. "You asked and I told you the way to do it. The fools running things took the bait and started bombing. Never work. FOOLS." He puts the Coke back by her locked hands.

Jen pushes the Coke away and says, "You overlook the many Arab nations and Islams opposing you. They have the ground forces needed to blast ISIS off the face of the Earth!"

Wolf smirks. "I doubt there is a charismatic leader, let alone military warrior, capable of rallying together a pan Arab movement to take us on. I doubt Abdullah will roll his dice to learn if he has the goods. Meanwhile, our brigands parade their Kurd captives in cages like scenes from HBO's Rome. We are today's Romans, baby."

Jen's fury is palatable. "How pathetic, burning a Jordanian pilot alive in a cage."

Wolf meets her intensity. "How many civilian women and children did he explode and burn with his bombs?"

Jen asks as a reply, "How much of this madness is just about OIL?"

Wolf again rises to the challenge. "The oil business morphed into the energy business. Yet, "Big Oil" appears to have hegemony in that mansion. Jasus H. Christ, Jen, think back to the early days of George W. Bush's presidency, those three days when the vice president, Halliburton Cheney, held private group meetings with the leaders of 'Big Energy.'"

Jen fires in with venom, "You're worse than Dick Cheney!"

Wolf laughs and storms on. "For better and for ugly, you Americans require and use enormous quantities of energy. Since World War I you've been an imperial power in the hands of oil. Oil men perceived themselves as ROYALTY, a follow-along in the mirror tradition of cattlemen. No accident that large-spread cowmen are called cattle barons. What followed in the minds of 'Big Energy' is 'What's Good for Enron is Good for Everybody,' Sugar Tits, does your Mustang define you as much as your blind veteran does? Here's a good one—the car most likely to be in a single-vehicle fatal accident is The Chevy

Camaro, an ill-designed, scape-built piece of unsafe shit. Or is it that the Camaro attracts male buyers who drive it recklessly, sometimes as a weapon? How do you drive that '66 classic of yours? I can see you cascading down Pennsylvania Avenue, never at speed limits. You're another oil guzzler, aren't you, babe? In winter, do you kick your thermostat up to seventy-six and sixty-eight in summer? Those are fucking luxury temps and luxury costs money. Luxury on this doomed planet always means some poor sucker doesn't get the same amount of choice per heating and cooling. This energy luxury requires source-dependency, interaction with Mohammedans, both Shi'ia and Sunni, none of whom like you."

Jen shakes her head and pleads, "Stop! Please stop! You exhaust me!"

Wolf rattles on. "They know foreigners, meaning infidels, despoiled their world and dismissed their assorted value. And when those 'bastards' as you see them get out of line, when you can't coddle them into compliance like the Saudis, you try to buy them. As a last resort, send in the Marines. Nothing's changed for a hundred years. Next comes your pipeline. Shouldn't the folks of the depopulated center of your country be able to prevent such a pipeline? Eminent Domain is the devil in the wings. Unless I help before then, the Pipeline will be an ecological disaster!"

Jen closes her eyes, overcome. She says, "You plan to kill me with words, is that it? Don't you need a break?"

Wolf smirks. "No, but, I am hungry. What would you like? Limited to McDonald's."

Jen opens her eyes. "Any one of you would be spotted by now. You've gone international."

Wolf shrugs. "The comrades are not advertised. Good, upstanding American citizen Muslims. I like your term, 'comrade.' Takes me back to the good ol' days."

Jen scoffs, "I bet. Fish sandwich, any small salad,

Ranch, I still have half this Coke left."

Wolf pulls out a small ring of keys, uses one to unlock her cuffs. "Take a nap before you eat."

Jen picks up the Coke and goes to her door when Wolf says, "Get some rest, toots. The best is yet to come."

CHAPTER SEVENTEEN

Inspire and Invent

Jen finishes neither the fish sandwich nor the blah salad. Quickly, eagerly, she removes the straw from her Coke, grabs the remains of the sandwich and salad, goes to the toilet, drops her pants and panties, and leans far back to the tank. First she twists one end of the plastic straw into a point. Using her teeth, she is able to tighten the point into a firm end, very much like a somewhat thickened needle. Carefully, adroitly, she chews bits of the fish and drops it morsel by morsel into the straw, intermingling it with both moist and coarse elements from the salad. It is time consuming and meticulous work. She glances at the Timex figuring she has to fashion this thing in no more than five minutes. When she reaches that point in time, she still has an inch or so to go. However, enough fish and organics remain to finish in about two more minutes.

Next, using her tongue and saliva, she wets the entire straw, which is now relatively firm. Carefully, she places the straw on the floor behind the stool. She makes certain her hands never lower in front of her legs. Her hope is that it will dry quickly and be cool enough there to gain more rigidity after several hours. She places the empty Coke cup and remainder of food on the edge of the cot, fakes wiping, flushes, pulls up her clothes, and back to the camera, mashes the cup and food containers into as neat a ball of garbage disposal as she can. Looking at it, not much is visible as a whole entity. With luck, they won't unwind the mess and discover the missing straw.

Jen reclines to get a little rest before being returned to the makeshift I-Compartment. She doesn't rest long.

Rahm returns smelling of chicken nuggets, a few still in a box in one of his hands. He motions her to sit at the table. Rahm goes back into her compartment, returning almost immediately with the ball of garbage. He places it on the table with his nuggets box. Carefully, always courteous, he locks the cuffs on her. She almost smiles when he pops the last nugget into his mouth, puts her garbage roll into his nuggets box, smashes it all together and exits into the rear compartment. She breathes deeply, relaxing.

Jen greets Wolf's return with a sharply edged question. "This sound familiar? 'Take off the cuffs, get me a flat white Starbucks, and let's really talk!'"

Wolf laughs, very relaxed, as he sits opposite her. "You haven't earned it yet. So what else have you determined?"

Jen decides to play along for a bit. "I know damn well you plan two strikes."

Wolf in standard form replies, "We do? Where?"

Jen decides to risk more, figuring she must be down to hours before he has to eliminate her. "Either a diversion, than something massive, or the big one and a follow-up to disrupt our retaliation."

Wolf grimaces and shrugs. "Decent analysis though wrong."

Jen retorts, "You expect me to see you acknowledge when I'm right? Keep in mind who we are, Wolf. We're not to be trusted."

Wolf just stares at her. She is even better than he believed. He decides to push a bit further. "Let's say you're relatively on target, where would we strike? When?"

The sharply tuned Jen knows he is flirting with disaster and so is she. She knows she has no choice but to follow his lead. "Oh, any large government or military facility as long as it is packed with sufficient and important persons, including the President."

Wolf lowers his gaze at her and replies, "And when?"

Jen realizes that if she shares too much conjecture and she's correct, she may shorten her life dramatically. She risks one more perceptive detail that has to be true. "The location will determine the point in time."

Wolf cannot help admire, and lets it be known. "You are good, really good. However, it now becomes a fierce guessing game, does it not?"

Jen risks shaking her head in defiance. "No. Your escape had to be timed for a reason. You're about to strike or you wouldn't be out."

At last Wolf relaxes and muses to himself. *Finally off track. The first hit will be diversion and in about eight months. The big strike in nine. I'm out now to make elaborate plans for safety between strikes plus the major exit plan after the big one.* He decides to relent and get her off topic. If he pushes further, she might strike gold via some tipoff from him in response.

He ponders to himself. *But what difference would it make now? She's done.* However, he now knows she is really good.

Wolf sips a hot caramel mocha, noting the Coke from her lunch still has ice with a lemon floating on top. He decides to return to one of the interests he has gleamed from her. "Why did you think I was into philosophy? Teaching one class to dumb freshmen is no big deal."

Puzzled by this tact, Jen responds, "You seem more taken with history but you wax philosophically about it. You still sound more American to me than Islamic, let alone ISIS. Something's fishy about your entire conversion. I don't really believe your adopted way of life. It merely suits your current state of negative apathy."

Wolf laughs, enjoying that response. "You think I'm just passing through a phase, eh? Keep in mind what al Baghdadi said, 'I'll see you in New York!' Jenny, you and Prez Dither remain defensive about Islam. Are you blind? Honey, your current problem ain't with Presbyterians."

Jen decides to fight, be assertive, get the conflict going in earnest. She is feeling reckless, sensing her own end. "Fuck your call to prayer! All that wailing and hooting. Let the Shi'ia and Sunni beat each other up endlessly! You'll all drown in your own blood!"

Wolf fights back. "Shit, I gave you a program to win, didn't I? Use General James Mattis and the First Marine Division with A-10 planes for close air support. No embedded idiot press. Just a ruthless march from Mosul to Damascus where you at least have mission-creep, topping off al Assad, He'd dash to Tehran doing eye exams from a hole-in-the-wall optometry office. Not only Prez Dither, but, the whole lot of Republican fools don't even see the simple plan that would work because no one wants another land war over there! What self-defeating bullshit! Maybe someone like Lindsay Graham or even the Benghazi dodging witch would get it done. McCain would have done it but he's so yesterday's newspapers he's ignored."

Jen snaps at him, "McCain's still around!"

Wolf doesn't even blink as he cascades on. "I remind you again, when Abu Bakr al-Baghdadi walked out of detention a few years ago he smiled at the last American soldier at the gate, chuckled, and said, 'See you in New York!' Sugar Tits, how did your prez, operating in a haze of confusion, respond to al-Baghdadi and his creation, the Islamic State, that is, the Caliphate in Syria/Iraq? He asked Congress to allow him to make a measure-by-measure response to barbarity. Good grief, Code Jen, what would Teddy Roosevelt have done? A strong President would have declared al-Baghdadi a 'Wanted Dead or Alive Criminal' and launched a program like I detailed to kill or capture every single ISIS supporter. You keep hearing your administration cry that you are not in a war with Islam! You aren't? Perhaps it's the Unitarians who want Sharia. Islam is not quite in a civil war. It would be an Islamic Civil War if the West was not the primary target. As it is, there's no sign of a major counter-response to Islamic Fundamentals. I embraced them somewhat arbitrarily, I admit. Anything beats your crumbling republic or democracy. To the Islamic people, the West is THE THING and ITS DOUBLE! Islamists want the benefits of wealth and your culture, but, they hate you, viscerally hate you, mostly for their own failures, for the abject failure of their religion, which they now can only cling to tightly and desperately."

Jen leaps into the fray as he pauses for breath. "What I see in the wealthier Muslim countries are too many people who have become what many Americans have become, morbidly obese slobs insisting on more whipped cream and chocolate sacrum for their ice cream 'n cookie-crumble cakes. Now I sound like you, don't I?"

They actually share a laugh and go silent for a moment. He is consciously aware of his growing attraction to her on more levels than one. She is aware of it, too, but, her life is at stake and she is fighting for it.

Jen continues. "America has its wacko religious nuts too. Go to Utah. Lovely little towns near red, rock mountains and green pastures. There are the folks who brought about the Mountain Meadows Massacre! And your last-ditch adoption puts you with Islam folks shouting, 'There is Only One God and Muhammad is His Prophet.' Ho, ho, ho. How about, "There is no God and All Prophets of Religion are Crazies!"

Wolf applauds lightly and leans toward her. "You are

really quite extraordinary. Any chance I'll convert you to our cause?"

Jen never blinks. "Not even to save my meaningless life."

"Well, Jenny Doll, better think about it. Time to sleep. We'll have one more day to chat. We better make it down an' dirty. I'll let you take educated guesses at targets. I promise to be honest since it won't make any difference whatsoever. Unless you decide to convert, of course. But then, how would you convince me when I trust no one?"

As he reaches the door, he turns to look at her. "Ahmed will bring you some homemade Arabic soup and a decent salad. His own dressing, delicious enough to be marketed wholesale."

Jen notes at once that Ahmed is wise in culinary arts.

Wolf continues. "Oh, might take the cuffs next time. Might not. When I took them off to send you back to pee, you behaved well, although I did find it tawdry that you ate while on the potty. As for today's game, almost a tie. I took the day by upending your Shakespeare quote. As for ISIS, looks like a problem inherited by the next President. And I do not refer to next year's election."

CHAPTER EIGHTEEN

Anatomy and Autonomy

Jen actually liked the superb soup and salad. Indeed the dressing was stunning. Could Ahmed have made that from scratch in their compartment? She marveled at the possibility.

She needed to nap, but used several reflective minutes to go over her training and knowledge of anatomy. Were she able to attack Wolf, an item for later planning or improvisation, she must consider the best soft targets on him for her makeshift weapon still cooling toward stability and use.

Forcing her mind to it, she recites to herself and visualizes: the carotid sinus arteries widen at their branch point in the neck, close to the trachea, windpipe. Unlikely she could also get to the larynx, voice box. That would be a major bonus because noise would alert the men at the back of the trailer. The femoral artery is in deep tissue. The internal jugular lies beneath the sternocleidomastoid muscle, lateral to the carotid arteries, whereas the external jugular lies on top of that muscle. She recalls work in the lab. She knows that the skin is by far the most resistant tissue, apart from bone or calcified cartilage. If her weapon can break through the skin on forcible push or thrust, no further force would be needed to cause rapid penetration of the tissues beneath the skin. If one presses or thrusts slowly, the skin will only "dimple in" like the effect of a weight on a trampoline. The initial strike of skin is the distinct threshold level between dimpling the skin and penetrating it. She smiles to herself recalling the doctor in the lab explaining that three kilograms or 1.1 pound of pressure is required to penetrate skin, up to as much as 6.6 pounds if the instrument is dull. However, if the weapon is moving at combat speed, accurate readings like that one are impossible to gauge. In other words, strike fast and hard, precisely on target. The key is the point of the plastic straw. She could easily dimple the skin on her arm with it as a test, a good sign it might work.

Most difficult to calculate was how long it would take for him to go unconscious or die if she can hit any one of the key arteries, all nicely close together. Ideally, hitting either jugular would be best, the external having less protection than the internal. A terrific strike would shock and spurt blood, enough to possibly muffle any sound. A twist of the weapon upon entrance increases the shock, same as when a bayonet is thrust up and into a kidney. The target screams like a pig without the twist and shock.

Alive or unconscious, a perfect strike could render a target unconscious in twenty to thirty seconds, dead in two or three minutes, maybe less if the heart is pounding and moving blood at an accelerated pace. However, how to have Wolf free of motion at the strike? Aye, there's the rub, the need for the next level of plan. Following that, dealing with the other three men. It is a daunting situation. However, it is the cliché in spades: a life or death matter. She leans back to doze.

Jen actually sleeps as the remainder of the night passes. She does not dream. The door opens. Rahm enters with a McDonald's cup of coffee, steam rising from the drink space. He sets it by the sink and holds out an Egg

McMuffin, wrapped. He offers it to her. "Breakfast?" Jen takes it, though not hungry after that small but delicious meal the night before.

Rahm hands her the coffee and exits as she thanks him. Alone, she nibbles at the McMuffin. Carrying the coffee with her, she sits on the toilet to appear to be using it. She smiles and thinks *tawdry indeed*. Leaning far back, she reaches down, locates the straw, and picks it up. She is pleased at how firm it is, though perhaps not firm enough to penetrate skin easily. Even if she succeeded in hardening it, would it work at all? She moistens it again and places it back on the cool floor. It cannot freeze, but, it might increase in rigidity.

In the rear compartment, Wolf addresses his compatriots. "Late tonight, I'll call Ashram for a report on road blocks. If there are none, we'll start back after midnight. You'll make Fogo on time easily. I have to get to the safe house in Maryland tomorrow night. I have about six months to finalize plans because Ashram needs time to secure the funds it will take to get the five of us safely out of the country."

Rahm asks, "What about the families of Pasha and Abdul?"

Wolf nods. "Of course. Everyone."

Faisal, normally quiet, asks, "Are strikes still set for late December and mid-January?"

Wolf frowns at that question and its near specificity. "Nothing's changed. Just keep that to yourselves."

Rahm decides to confront the current issue. "The woman? Here? Today?"

Silence hangs in the air for a moment as Wolf looks away, then nods. "Just before we depart tonight."

Recognizing that something is not asked but in the air, Wolf adds, "No worry. I'll do it." The two men seem relieved but try not to reveal it.

After an uneasy moment, Wolf says to Rahm, "Time for

the final game. She's great for keeping me mentally sharp for intricate planning. Hell, maybe I'll spare her to keep me alert over the rest of the planning months."

The men stare incredulously at Wolf. He laughs, waving an arm. "Just kidding, men, just kidding. Put her in there without cuffs." Rahm does not move, staring at Wolf. He is no longer jocular. "You heard me. No cuffs."

Wolf resents Rahm's hesitation even if legitimate. Rahm exits.

Wolf finishes his drink. Faisal is lying down on his cot looking at an old *Sports Illustrated* issue.

Rahm returns, nods, sits, and opens *USA Today*.

Wolf exits into the middle compartment. Jen is still standing. He closes the door behind him and looks at her. Both are expressionless as their eyes meet.

Finally Wolf pulls back his chair, sits, and plants his Tony Lama boots on the desk, tilting the chair back at an angle. He tilts his Stetson down over his eyes and waits.

Jen speaks as she sits. "Starting without cuffs is ominous. I assume we won't be long."

Wolf pushes the Stetson back and smiles. "To the contrary. Today will be our last chance for fun and games. We can take as long as we want. Lunch will come on time. We'll take a break, then finish up."

Jen nods. "I see."

Wolf's favorite question. "Do you?"

Jen ignores his rhetorical nonsense and asks, "Where do we start? How?"

Wolf pulls his feet down, sitting up. "This morning, let's dismiss all the pertinent topics at issue. After lunch, I promise, we'll get past the games to the heart of the matter. I'll give clues to test your final acuity. If you pass, you'll know everything."

"And take it to my grave," Jen adds without expression. Wolf responds, "I am curious. Burial or cremation?"

Jen doesn't miss a beat. "Cremation."

"Ahhh," Wolf sighs. "Then no grave."

Jen says, "No. Into the Pacific at Moss Beach in Laguna. It's a family thing."

Wolf stares at her. He is struggling against conflicting desires and knows it. After a moment, he says, "Your stupid, reckless congressional Democrats released a "torture" report recently, a report written without testimony from the guy who ran your interrogation program. Perhaps you're familiar with that program, maybe graduated from it?"

Jen does not move or say a word. Wolf goes on.

"The report opened a grotesque, violent Pandora's Box internationally with Americans attacked hither and yon. The Democratic Party won't recover for a dozen years, if it ever does recover. What do you think about Prez Dither then sending a squad of Guantanamo sludge heads to Uruguay to become immigrants?"

Jen replies, "I approve."

Wolf smiles. "Good. Me too. If our men find their way back into mischief in Syria or Iraq faster than a small town rumor, so be it, eh? Your prez acted in the spirit of Lincoln. There, see, I can praise as well as condemn."

Jen glares at him and says, "Wolf, you're crazier than a stomped possum."

Wolf roars with full out delighted laughter. "Way to go, Sugar Tits. Now you're thinking and talking like me!" She smirks this time as he finishes laughing.

Their eyes meet in silence again. He says quietly, "You are as attractive in the morning as evening."

Jen replies, "All the same to me, means nothing."

Wolf nods. "Yes, I see that, dear. When did passion die in you?" No reply. He adds, "Perhaps in the arms of your sightless Marine?"

Jen's voice rises just a tad. "This approach is pointless and you know it. Might as well talk about Russia."

Wolf shrugs. "Fine. For now, Russia. Which means,

Putin. He'll likely have another decade in power, proceeding in perceptions and delusions. Putin sees America correctly as in decay, gone soft, half-bankrupt, incapable of sustained sacrifice for anyone or anything. Prez Dither scolds Putin over human rights and Ukraine, Putin sneers and continues."

Jen jumps into the screed. "We have sanctions!"

Wolf laughs and continues. "Sanctions? They do damage but take too long. Watch for more Russian incursions and muscle flexing. Bomber flights into the Caribbean come next. Putin, a former KGB lifer, sees human and international interaction as based on both actual and implied power. He's stripped himself or hidden away anything and anyone who might make him vulnerable. He's as alone in the Kremlin as Dither is in the White House. These two men are complete unto themselves, needing no friends or buddies. Dither has far more personal weaknesses, vulnerabilities. Putin has never allowed his wife a public, a platform. Like a mob boss, Putin set his daughter aside into a protective cocoon. Putin has evolved into an Orthodox monk, a desert father of the sort Thomas Merton wrote about. An isolate, a solitary, lots of self-discipline. He's the product of history or history as he perceives it from his stance, as well as from Russian collective memory. Remember, Jen, Russia has always been under threat of invasion. The Czarist/Stalinist strategy requires buffers against prospective invasion. Of course, the Mongols rode into Moscow and sacked it. Putin knows how close Hitler's army came to Moscow. By the way, did you know that George Orwell confessed that he had never been able to dislike Hitler? Orwell had reviewed Mein Kampf and was attracted to Hitler's underdog quality. Your best scholars today correctly recognize that the Islamic State partisans have the same appeal."

Jen jumps in saying, "Since we're at the eleventh hour

of our affair, when you finish your punditry of Russia, explain ISIS and this Islamic State to me, this Caliphate or Khilafah."

"Happy to oblige, love. We'll soon get to the really big issues. However, no question, Russia and Putin will be interesting in the immediate years ahead. And a quick word about your flock of would-be leaders who will have to oppose him. Jeb Bush scrambles for the middle while Rand Paul offers neo-centrism. Ted Cruz is a Joe McCarthy style Republican.

"Guv Walker will kill his own chances after he destroys a once great university system. Guv Kristie will bully himself into a corner. Dr. Carson is certifiable. Hillary will come across as brittle and shrill. Joe Biden will slip into dementia. Your friends and neighbors will elect a president based on what Grizzly Mom Palin ridiculed as the 'hopey-changey thing.' Democrats have no Jimmy Carter to rise out of southern obscurity."

Wolf pauses. Jen has not moved, hands clasped together on the table.

He leans back and asks, "Jasus Syphilitic Christ, woman, no retort on Russia? Putin? Dither? The lost leaders of both parties?"

Jen sighs. "I'm impressed. I can't counter those arguments."

He stares at her, caught off guard. He wonders what in hell she is doing? Is this somehow an escape plan? Silence and complicity? Yet she baits him about the Islamic State and Khilafah. He decides to put that major issue aside and try another approach. He knows he is playing toward seduction of one kind or another. He cannot resist. Wolf resumes with new energy. "You admire my western gear, I can tell. Are you into western music? Art? Poetry?"

Jen smiles, unclenches her hands, and leans back. "Enlighten me."

Some strange, desperate urge is stirring in her too,

but she hasn't time to figure it out. Survival? A plan? She dismisses it in the face of his new energy and subject.

Wolf plunges onward. "I used to write open field projective verse, prosody promoted by the folks who were at now-extinct Black Mountain College years ago. You know, '30s-50s?"

She doesn't know but nods. He seems suddenly like an enthusiastic boy to her. Fascinating.

Wolf is up, pacing. "Painters like Josef Albers, Robert Motherwell, Willem de Kooning. Poets like Charles Olson, Robert Creeley, Ed Dorn. I knew Dorn long ago. He evolved into a fine western writer, poet, with his 'Gunslinger' poems. Men like Tom Clark had no advanced degree to land a solid tenure-track teaching sinecure at some posh university. Clark was too wild and singular in his youth. Now he's in his toothless, crippled seventies his body ravaged by age and illness."

Jen just stares at him, but she is suppressing something akin to admiration.

His excitement is growing as he continues. "The Black Mountain poets influenced the Beats, the New York School and L=A=N=G=U=A=G=E poetry, like the Pulitzer Prize poetess, Rae Armantrout, in an M.A. creative writing program at San Francisco State. Envoy is intended as direct address to readers, being more formal that conversational upon completion of a poem. It's an ancient convention, Jen. Poets today use Envoy in poems. Irish poet, Thomas MacDonagh, is one. He was one of the sixteen leaders of the 1916 Irish Rising. His best works are translations MacDonagh made of poems by Sappho. His son became a jurist and writer, too."

Suddenly Wolf stops. He looks at her. "Sorry. A little carried away."

Jen says softly, "Frustrated poet, western? It becomes you."

Wolf retreats. "Flattery will get you everywhere. Okay,

You pick a subject, but save the gut stuff about ISIS strikes 'til later. Maybe after I explain ISIS and Khilafah to you, we can elope and watch the world end together."

Jen pushes her luck by saying, "Time is precious, let's cut to the chase."

Wolf pauses and says coldly, "We still have time to kill. Now name a subject."

Jen leans forward and says, "Israel."

Wolf chuckles. "That won't take long. The Israeli's are faced with what today is correctly referred to as an existential threat. The Persians have vowed over and over to destroy Israel. Why not believe the Persians? And Persians never cease negotiating but never in good faith. Bear in mind, the final say in Tehran is with the Ayatollah, not with elected officials and certainly not with the negotiators. Netanyahu bellows on about this because Prez Dither has been far less of a friend to Israel that they would have liked."

He pauses. "Questions? Rebuttal? Well, then, match to Wolf. Another subject?"

Jen flashes awareness. *He's deliberately putting this off. He has to kill me and he doesn't want to do it. He's too proud to ask one of the comrades to do it.* Grasping at a straw, she announces, "The American Sniper and ground troops!"

Now it is Wolf who doesn't miss a beat. "That fucked up movie is a success due to easy patriotism. A movie ticket costs about the same as an American flag auto decal. The truth is you Americans don't want your sons let alone your daughters playing out the sniper role in reality in a bomb-shaken building in Aleppo. You don't want to do what it would take to defeat us or even Al Qaeda. You absolutely don't want your children taking on the regular Russian army in eastern Ukraine. Who the hell knows what that sniper movie is about. I'd never see such propaganda because it would remind me of John Wayne, Steven

Seagal, Charles Bronson, Sylvester Stallone, and, above all, Clint Eastwood, who directed this thing. I suppose there's a revenge/vengeance theme to the popularity, like the peevish mood that propels certain quarters of the White American Film Industry. The only thing worse is the string of redundant, mindless musicals and comedies that poured out of the Golden Age of Hollywood."

Jen blurts a retort, "Hollywood? Now you sound like a bitter movie critic!"

He shrugs and continues. "The same thing is found in the dozens and dozens of Shakespeare Festivals in this country where the masses go for culture. Then there's Broadway. The Jews and homosexuals allow very few gentiles and straights to spoil their party. To think of America's youths as the boots on the ground Fox news calls for, you would have to pull soft pottery artistes off their clay wheels, sending them shit-scared to Mosul to use a laser pen to pain a target. Won't happen. You'll have to rely on other Muslins to do the job for you which is equally hopeless. Jordan King Abdullah, a cosmopolitan of the West with a lovely estate in England, is no Warrior King. Yes, he SHOULD be. I told you, he's the forty-first direct fucking descendant of the Prophet Muhammad and the grandson or great grandson of Lawrence of Arabia's warrior-king pal, King Faisal. This Jordan hero today was born to rule despite being, by blood, something like half-British, educated in posh English and American schools. Those schools produced grand poets like Robert Lowell but no inspirational generals like Mattis or MacCrystal." Wolf pauses. "Why are you fidgeting? Too much enlightenment?"

Jen stands up briskly. "I have to pee."

Wolf points to her door. "Go then. Tell you what, take a break. I have a few things to do."

He looks at his watch, an expensive military type. He speaks to her in an almost friendly manner.

"Later in the afternoon, Rahm will bring you a combination lunch/dinner. Then you and I will wrap things up into the evening, our second as you undoubtedly figured out. And our last. We're almost there, Jen. Point of no return."

In her compartment Jen sits on the toilet. Her brain is racing as she continues planning. Reaching the straw, she finds it firm. Firm enough to be of any use remains unclear. Carefully, she places it inside her blouse, at her side, the sharp tip tucked comfortably beneath her bra strap.

The blunted, flat bottom cannot poke her. Now for the rest of the plan.

CHAPTER NINETEEN

Facts and Fiction

A few hours pass as she finalizes a simple strategy and tactic. It will require getting very close to him, then targeting him perfectly. She knows the precise spot on his neck, a bit to the left of front. That is what chills her to the soles of her feet. She has never killed. She knows how to kill. She is trained to kill. Above all, can she kill this man? Is she certain he will kill her if she does not? Worst, what will he do if she doesn't kill him?

At that moment Rahm actually knocks. She smiles. They must enjoy it when I hit the toilet even though robbed of full view. He motions her into the I-Compartment. Upon entering, Jen sees that he has placed Chicken McNuggets, small fries, three cookies, and her large Coke with lemon next to the cuffs. Wolf has not moved from the table.

He looks up at her and says, "Back to reliable McDonald's. Rahm has other things to do beyond his kitchen skills."

Wolf is finishing a Big Mac. Jen sits and looks at the cuffs. He smiles and says, "Just eat."

Silently they do so, finishing with fries. Deliberately, she shares hers with a nod and he accepts. They also share a small dollop of catsup on a wrapper. Jen offers him one of the cookies and he accepts it. The oatmeal raisin one, damn it. Her favorite.

Finally Wolf speaks. "Indeed, time to give you a short lesson on ISIS and the Islamic State. Isn't it shocking, Sugar Tits, that network and cable news units do not really grasp what is happening or why. Worse, your administration, congress, and government overall don't either. Some of your military get it, but, they're up against a progressive, peace oriented Prez Dither. And he's a hypocrite with his drone murders."

He pauses, chewing. "Damn good cookie. Almost like mama used to bake on Sunday mornings."

Jen picks up on that immediately. "Where was that, San Francisco or are you confusing her with your wife in Nebraska?"

Wolf smiles. "Oh, it was mama all right, the day when our cook was off."

Jen asks, "Did mama also cook the meals on Sunday?"

Wolf chuckles. "Hell no. She ordered in but she was in her cups by then."

Jen persists. "Is that why your father left for Texas?"

Wolf quickly shuts the subject down. "He was a road warrior long before that. End of story."

He brushes off cookie crumbs and announces, "ISIS AND THE KHILAFAH!" Jen leans back, sipping her Coke through a straw, slyly moving it within her fingers for the best grip, preparing for later.

Wolf is in a good mood, pleased by the subject. "The Islamic State is also known as the Islamic State of Iraq and al-Sham, some say, Syria. Hence, ISIS. Some say, ISIL, but, we prefer ISIS. Our belief is based on the path to the Day of Judgment. All operations and operatives tend to the strategy of reaching that day. The major mistake of the West is to see jihadism as monolithic, applying the same logic of Al Queda to ISIS when we have far eclipsed those lesser fighters. Americans tend to date things from

9/11. Osama bin Laden used that day as prologue to a caliphate he knew he'd never live to see. The Islamic State requires territory only to appear legitimate. We use a diffuse network of autonomous cells."

Jen dares to interrupt. "Your own cell being prominent in America."

Wolf tilts his head some and replies, "It will be, yes. Please don't interrupt. You'll have a chance to question and challenge."

He clears his throat and continues. "Had you and most Americans read Graeme Wood's reporting and writing about us you would have been far more knowledgeable. Your most secular authority on us is Bernard Haykel, a genuinely smart-ass professor. Relying on someone like Joe Biden or Hillary Clinton is laughable. CNN reporter, Peter Bergen, at least interviewed bin Laden in 1997 and came to understand that OF COURSE THIS IS A HOLY WAR! IT IS PRECISELY WHAT DITHER REFUTES. All that happens today, highlighted by beheading and burning people alive is strictly out of our medieval religious nature. We are following that which our books and prayers demand, the slaughter of non-believers, the infidels. It is written that we will end up fighting a huge army, labeling it simply as 'Rome.' That army could be yours or the amalgamation of what Prez Dither is trying to coalesce. 'Rome' could be Italy or it could be any huge battlefield in Europe or the Middle East. We will then rule the world, including the United States or perish with the end of Earth itself."

Content, Wolf relaxes. "Go ahead. Questions, challenges?"

Jen leans forward. "Is Osama bin Laden still the key modern figure in all this madness?"

Wolf smiles and replies, "He is Sheikh Osama, honored with that title and revered. He corporatized terror and franchised it out as both Wood and Haykel recognized. None of your leaders pay attention to those two men.

Sheikh Osama wanted specific concessions, such as the withdrawal of your forces from Saudi Arabia. He organized foot soldiers. They were educated but common men, true Islamics. On Mohammed Atta's last day of life, before taking off at Logan in Boston, anxious to divert the flight to the Trade Center in New York, he shopped at Walmart and ate dinner at Pizza Hut."

Jen laughs in spite of herself. Wolf responds. "Yes, it's laughable. However, our leaders are derisive about these 'moderns.' We don't waver from governing precepts embedded in Islam by the Prophet Muhammad and his earliest followers. We tend to speak in codes and allusions that sound old fashioned to young followers at first. However, they come to honor the old traditions and texts of early Islam. We urge Muslims in Western countries to find an infidel and kill him or her. We urge poison, bullets, knives, fire, stoning, crop destruction, and bombing."

Jen stands as she says, "Like you're planning!"

Wolf snaps at her, "Sit down!" She stares at him but does not move. Wolf smiles, adding softly, "Please."

Her mind is racing now, aware that time is running short. Jen complies.

She is shocked but hides it when Wolf reaches forward to idly pat her folded hands. He says, "We're getting down to it now. Any other questions about the Islamic State?"

Jen shakes her head. "No, I think I get it fully now. That was very helpful, not that some of us didn't already understand. It's so ancient and pagan, you surely see why it's so difficult for Christians or anyone else, including modern Muslims, to grasp the barbaric aspects of this thing."

Wolf nods. "Yes, I do understand. However, it explains why so many fine, well educated youngsters from fine, modern households feel alienated and lost. ISIS offers a chance to count, to oppose the chaos, find a purpose indeed, find an identity."

Jen nods. "As a brutal killer."

Wolf retorts, "As a WARRIOR FOR ALLAH!" They stare into each other's eyes. Sensing he might be breaking through to her, Wolf continues. "Do you see now why the new Iraq army turned tail and ran from ISIS? Those weak souls betrayed your government and military, betrayed all your many dead Americans who died over there for absolutely nothing. The new Iraq army you trained so well, ho ho, ceded Sunni Iraq military vehicles, arms and ammunition to the Caliphate. The capable army of Saddam Hussein was actually professional and capable. Most Americans now realize that George W. and Cheney destroyed a nation that was better off with a tyrant.

"When they dismissed Hussein's generals and troops, they had no place to go except start ISIS. The fault lies not in the stars, Antony, but yourselves. Tyrant Hussein would have never allowed ISIS to grow and thrive. In the process, W. and Cheney also destroyed the entire foundation of your country. Prez Dither had no chance to restore it, though he obviously had the right ideas and tried. The ship had already sailed. And sunk. Now, last chance, honey. Join us?"

Jen wonders if this is a possible avenue into somehow finding a way to still stop this creature. She knows she must be very careful. He is way beyond any adversary she ever met or even dreamed of meeting. She refuses to think of the burden she likely carries in saving her country from far worse disasters than 9/11. Finally, she speaks.

"Wolf, I prefer Sam, look, 'Sam,' I don't deny the power of your argument. You've a superb grasp of the fundamentals of the path you've chosen. If I were to say I'm at least in awe if not convinced, you wouldn't believe me anyway."

Wolf stares at her, weighing her words, her tone, her being. Could she possibly be sincere? He rejects it, but he realizes he considered the chance of it happening for a moment. He sits back and replies, "Try me. Convince me."

Jen asks carefully, "I was unaware of Wood and Haykel, but, I've read The Clash of Civilizations."

Wolf nods. "Ah, yes, Samuel P. Huntington. He saw the truth, that a war with Islam was inevitable."

Jen continues. "Yes, but this clash is exacerbated by resource scarcity, overpopulation, human migration, global warming, technological disruptions."

Wolf responds. "Of course, but, tolerance as a reality and social goals are eroding away in American and you know it. With major domestic attacks here, your populace will panic and collapse. You no longer have the will for massive mobilization. Even if you did, you could never sustain it. You seem to conquer Iraq and Afghanistan then pull out too soon. Your country cannot endure the economic erosion of another long period of war."

Jen quips, "Well, Wolf, we're modern."

He snorts and blathers on. "You've left the 19th Century, you've buried your best and ancient 'Best Generation' that won World War II. America is not Sparta. It's not even Athens. Your president is feared by no one and is what he wishes to see in his mirror. He may be better than the cross-dressing, perpetual orgies of a gay Roman boy-Emperor like Eligabula, but he's no match for our Islamic State. You people have mollycoddled your kids, socially promoted them, told them their quirks and fatal flaws are really bases of social acceptability and celebration. You're graduating physically and intellectually unfit kids from your schools All public schools are a sham, a mess. Your colleges graduate people with less than high school level reading skills. Your graduate schools are self-serving perverts. You do not want war with ISIS unless it's a Hollywood movie that can be won in two hours by George Clooney and Brad Pitt. ISIS loves filmmaking. Look how good we are at staging, costuming, total theatrics. More and more Muslims have chosen the satisfactions they find in the Koran. With your unique intellect and gifts as a woman, you should join us." He eyes her carefully.

Jen knows she is walking on proverbial eggshells, if not hot coals. She decides to play him a little further while she can find an actual opportunity. As yet, she remains lost in the compressed circumstances of her kidnapping and this strange prison on wheels.

She speaks softly. "My father was an honorable military man when our country was glorious, after Korea." She puts that comment out and carefully observes his eyes. He shows no emotion but replies at once, a man of history and knowledge at all times.

"Jen, you may be right from Truman to Eisenhower, even Kennedy, with all his flaws. From Lyndon Johnson on, steady decline. Had LBJ gone into Viet Nam with overwhelming force from the outset, as he was advised by his generals, he might have succeeded. On the other hand, even if he had just ended the war and got out he might be remembered as a great leader because of his domestic and civil right achievements, no matter that he didn't personally believe in all of them. LBJ still got things done 'til Viet Nam and Bobby Kennedy fucked him up. Jasus H. Christ, agent Code Jen, the Commandant of the Marine Corps, David Shoup, a Medal of Honor recipient, said from the initial placement of military advisers in Nam that is was a dirty money-grubbing war, one that would benefit only those Eisenhower had warned against, the 'Military-Industrial Complex." Had either Kennedy or Johnson accepted the offer from retired Marine Corps General Lewis 'Chesty' Puller, you might have won that war. Puller was the most decorated Marine in history. He said that had he been given the First Marine Division and close air support, he would have marched to Hanoi in two weeks' time, burned it to the ground, and marched out. It was the slow escalation of war that guaranteed it would turn into a quagmire Americans perceived as an immoral defeat.

Once again, you have a leader who wants to fight ISIS piecemeal. Former President Carter, Secretaries Clinton, Panetta, Gates and National Security Adviser General Jim Jones have spoken the truth to Prez Dither's deaf ear. No one paid proper attention to General Stan MacCrystal's cutting interview for ROLLING STONE magazine because it was foolish to speak out in print. A Harvard JFK School of Government Dean and CNN pundit, David Gergen, said on national television that Dither operates in 'a haze of confusion.' Your prez is a quasi-intellectual whereas you're a genuine one. The man is bright enough to be a true intellectual but he's not academically thorough. He's like Tricky Dick Nixon in one aspect. He makes up his mind, then requires that his advisers find the evidence necessary to back him up. He's a professor-posturing fellow. He reminds me more and more of a character from a Samuel Beckett play called All Strange Away. The stage direction goes, 'Have him say no sound. No way in, none out, he's not here.'"

Silence. Jen is suffering because she is actually in awe of this son of a bitch. She decides to protest, but mildly. "Well, there are some fine people in his cabinet, damn it."

Wolf snorts. "Not for long. Secretary Hagel, vocally frustrated with the president, is micro-managed into paralysis. Another Defense Secretary is fired, bites the dust. Ted Williams would say, 'Jesus syphilitic Christ!'"

Jen snaps back, "I thought it was Jasus, not Jesus and who's Ted Williams, an actor?"

Wolf smiles and shakes his head. "Oh, darling, you are out of touch, fine intellect or not. Teddy Fucking Ballgame! The Splendid Splinter! Best hitter major league baseball ever saw!"

Jen retorts, "Really? Did you play with him? You say you caught Bob Feller."

Wolf laughs out loud. "Yes, I did, Durham Bulls, baby! No, I never played with Ted but I saw him hit in a game once. Bee-Utiful!"

Jen relaxes. "I'll take your word for it."

Wolf counters, "You better hurry up and take more than my word for it."

Jen swallows as her mind races. *I need a break to think this further.* She asks quietly, "How about a short break? It must be early evening. A potty break, then maybe strong coffee?"

He stares at her quietly, reminding himself harshly that she is the enemy despite every other instinct in him. He nods. "We'll take a break. I'll send Ahmed to Starbucks. Special treat for our last session. Flat white?"

For a second Jen stares at him, briefly stunned by his reference to a comrade by name. She thinks intentional, he's past caring. *I'm down to a couple hours at best.* She nods assent to the cappuccino.

As Jen enters her compartment at the front of the trailer, she shudders, leaning back against the door. The clock in her head is ticking. She gently touches that straw.

CHAPTER TWENTY

'Leventh and Last

In D.C. Dan finds himself talking aloud to Smokey, his loyal companion. Dan has never been so worried let alone depressed. He knows that Jen is as capable as a human being could be in her situation, but Dan also realizes she is up against a man worse than just another ISIS killer. All reports indicate a particularly cunning man with spurious wealth and support behind him. His escape alone signaled a man with international power. While nothing was mentioned in press releases, his private audience with the FBI Director clarified for Dan that the country is in great danger, not just the woman he loves. All he can do now is wait and count on Smokey for sight and solace.

* * *

At that moment Jen is summoned back to the Interrogation compartment in the trailer by Rahm who dutifully hands her the Flat White, extra hot, steaming cup from a nearby Starbucks. He says not a word and leaves. Jen sits to sip the drink, happy to remain out of the cuffs.

Wolf enters with an extra hot cinnamon Dolce Latte, sits, and continues to speak as if there had been no interruption.

"It's good to know we're aware of the better writers and thinkers on our subjects. Well, at least I'm aware. You have some catching up to do, hon. I forgot to ask you if you know Robert D. Kaplan's, The Coming Anarchy? In his summary, Kaplan underscores the fact that peace, as a primary goal, is dangerous because it implies that you will sacrifice any principle to get it. Jen, you and I know the world is not a benign place."

Jen pings in at him. "Not with you in it!"

Wolf grins and nods, pushing on. "Your country has had a relatively peaceful turf, 9/11 notwithstanding, because you've had superior weaponry. However, Sam Huntington again is worth noting. Western ideas of individualism, liberalism, constitutionalism, human rights, equality, liberty, the rule of law, democracy, free markets, and separation of church and state, have little resonance in Islamic, Confucian, Japanese, Hindu, Buddhist, or Orthodox cultures. Your values and ideas are not universal! Conflict is inevitable!"

Jen feels overwhelmed as though trying to take notes from a genius and intimidating professor in a defeated tutorial. She tries to fight back.

"You Islamists are like the new Caliph in Syria-Ambar. Hunkered down crazed as a subway rat in bright sunlight in al-Baghdadi."

Wolf smiles, loving her response. He senses some parity which is exactly what he yearns for compared to the men in his quartet cell.

He responds, "Yes, we keep dividing and dividing again. After the latest rocket from Gaza, right on the eve of the tenth anniversary of Arafat's death by poisoning, Hamas and Fatah are bombing the homes of each party's leaders. Persian meddling helps the abject collapse of Prez Dither's hopes. Make a deal with the Persians on nuclear matters? The Israeli's dare not trust any such deal.

Ever hear of Fouad Ajami, from The Dream Palace of the Arabs? 'A country's myth can console and knit together men and women of different needs, carry them through difficult times, explain sorrow and defeat, locate them in the world. But the myth can also hide a country from itself, hide it from scrutiny.' Fouad warned that world leaders perceive Prez Dither as weak and that despots believe he can be painlessly ignored. I'm reminded of Norman Mailer's revisit of his pre-1960 election canonization of John F. Kennedy. The essay was called "Superman Comes to the Supermarket." By 1963 Mailer took apart assumptions he made of JFK, his old Harvard classmate, seeing the president as mortal with major flaws. Let me shock you. I voted for Prez Dither in '08! I did so knowing I was voting for 'Jimmy Carter Lite.'"

Jen interrupts with irritation, "Another GOOD man, fine statesman!"

Wolf retorts, "But a poor president!" He continues, relentless, "I'd been conditioned by my revulsion and loathing for Republican/banker/ financial market greed. Today, I see the entire thing as rotten. I had no choice but to turn Islamic ISIS." He stares at her. She stares back.

Jen does not back down. "Your reading, labeling, name calling is a symptom of intellectual bankruptcy."

Wolf is pleased by her rejoinder and continues. "Jen, if you want to declaim about politics, particularly foreign affairs, you could have at least read Foreign Affairs magazine over the past decade. You could have been conversant with Kaplan, Huntington, even Senators McCain and Graham who have been correct about what you consider your theo-mad Islamic adversaries. Those two were right about Iraq, Afghanistan, Sudan, Syria, and Yemen. I'm trying to save your life here by getting you to see the world as it is, not as you and Dither wish it to be. Mine is a simple request from the ghost of Machiavelli. If he lives, a big 'if,' let your prez retire into a funded chair, a lovely professorship at a grand place like Harvard's JFK School of Government. Let him grind out books of bathetic self-justification."

Jen hangs in there saying, "You no longer live up to your western apparel. You now look and sound like a far-right conservative."

Wolf laughs, but he is irritated. "Well, baby, Johnny Cash and Waylon Jennings are dead. Merle Haggard must be eighty. My music is disappearing. Age will also work against Hillary and V.P. Biden. They won't be as telegenic as their adversaries. Allow me to finalize the current American political scene if only to shut you up metaphorically before I have to do it literally."

Jen shivers but steels herself and glares at him as he whirls onward.

"I once went to a Toyota dealership and met a car salesman who had once been a junior high school teacher. His name was Bruce. His hair was Elvis-black. He sold me a stodgy, mid-road Camry. I had wanted a cut-price Avalon, entry-level luxury rig. Bruce said to me, 'I don't like the Avalon, reminds me too much of the big four-door Cadillacs old people used to drive.' I told Bruce that I WAS one of those fucking people whose well-being is fucking enhanced by driving some big-ass, heated-seats fucking Cadillacs, or, at least a goddamned Toyota thirty-grand Avalon. The point of this story, honey, is that everyone in this mess of a country looks for a presidential candidate who's like a four-door Caddy. In that way, Jeb Bush would make sense but his wife is a fucking shopaholic. What a White House disaster that would be. No more Bushes, please. Bob Kerry can no longer win an election, too unconventional a mind. However, he was a fine university president at The New School. Jerry Brown's too old now."

Jen protests, "No, he is not!"

Wolf shakes his head in disappointment and turns to the military. "You might try another general. However,

Petraeus is apology-staggered after getting well laid by a hot journalist. MacCrystal had the Rolling Stone fiasco interview. He might serve at CNN as an analyst. Clearly, the Democratic field is open for a young, new voice. In time, sure, Liz Warren or some governor-like Jim Webb. The Democratic Party focuses on cheery attention to minorities, illegal aliens, and gays. That means the loss of more house and senate seats. With terms like 'Polar Vortex' entering the vocabulary, what terrible plagues, storms, and crises will humanity soon face? Look west at China with its needs, its perceptions. The next prez will constantly face off with China unless ISIS can save him and all of you from it. If oil prices stay down, watch out for Russia and Putin's oligarchy."

Jen almost shouts, "Blah, blah, blah!"

His eyes narrow but he forges on. "Putin's playing a long game but his demographics are against him. Just think, Jen, Henry Kissinger is really old. Evil as he was in many ways. he understood the global need or order, for rules both explicit and implicit, the classical Greek need for balances. Meantime, Prez Dither sends fucking LETTERS about ISIS to the Ayatollah in Iran! Jasus Syphilitic Christ, professor-in-chief is up to his third letter to the old raghead. The Ayatollah replied to the first letter with a pedantic scolding, paranoid screed. The second letter was ignored. Oh, and watch that slick Senator Rand Paul. He's putting less gel in his curly hair. That means he has an advisory team. They want him to avoid personal aberrations, like saying vaccinations can cause mental illness. Paul is trying to locate a way to feed his off-the-wall thinking into the political center. Jeb Bush is already au currant center. Hillary will be a pincushion for her rivals."

Jen is beginning to panic in her mind and guts. "Can we get down to our conflict, yours and mine?"

Wolf dislikes giving control over to anyone, least of all Jen. "Yes, but you will have to own your selfish, crazed ambition to do so. You will genuinely have to match or surpass me. It's time for Camus-centered existentialism. Are you up to the new stars of existential angst, sex, love, betrayal through abandonment and despair? Are you another Julia Cordeanu, Anais Nin, Milan Kundera? Let me see your real passion, Jen. I am no lover from a Leonard Cohen song, though Cohen studied poetry with Irving Layton, a world-class womanizer. Before we get to the showdown on what I am up to and your efforts to grasp it, we must erase the last of our political, philosophical debate, a debate I win over and over. It's a shame you never read Fouad Ajami's Dream Palace of the Arabs. He was once at Johns Hopkins with the dangerous neo-con, Paul Wolfowitz. Fouad is now at Stanford's Hoover Institute. Impressive, no?"

Jen laughs and cracks, "Not as impressive as you, of course!"

Wolf repeats, "Of course." He doesn't miss a beat and races on, sensing some finality descending on them. "Fouad's too much of a Shi'ia to be totally accurate, but he's right that the Arab house divides and subdivides. Despite Hussein in Jordan hanging on to power, the Hashamites are exhausted by history. Iraq will always be in some sort of civil war. Lebanon seethes. You don't have the culture or will to tame Mesopotamia the way the Roman Emperor Trajan did. Nor the brutal ways of the Mongolian hordes to cope with Persia. You have Dither and Hillary and their clown opposite Dennis Rodman."

Jen sighs, glancing at her Timex. "It's late afternoon. Let ME summarize your screed for you! Otherwise, we'll never get to it!"

Taken off guard, Wolf laughs and sits back. "Go for it, Code Jen."

Jen never raises her voice but makes her points. "You see our president as an adorable pound kitty named Friendless. That is narrow and glib, stupid."

Wolf chuckles, she goes on. "In the fall mid-term elections, it was disappointment and disillusionment with our kitty that caused the Republican landslide."

Wolf nods, enjoying this. She moves on snappily. "You believe Americans expect too much from the man and limit his legacy to Benghazi, no bankers in jail, Big Pharmacy run wild, a bumbling Affordable Care Act, no strategy, just tactics, with your Islamic State. Pandering to the riots of Ferguson. You view our president and our country as one stinky, leaky, subcutaneous anal cyst. You see Hillary as a woman overcome by the love-eager plump girl at the end of the rope line in her beret. You quote Samuel Beckett at will, 'the great bottom foams into stillness.' You attack our presidents but not as roughly as they attacked Lincoln. You want to kill him really, rather than allow a good, sweet, decent man take retreat on the golf links of Palm Springs. I predict to you, sir, that our president will live out his term, defeat you and your Islamic State, retire, and one day be appointed to the United States Supreme Court. Republicans in 2034 will briefly filibuster against that nomination, but they will be brought to shame for this and he will become our Supreme Court Chief Justice."

Wolf suddenly explodes in admiration, "Wow! Go, girl, go!"

"Wolf, surely you see how desperate your clan is when they resort to raising money by harvesting organs from its victims. Twenty-three Iraqi Christians AND doctors allegedly refused to butcher the recent dead so they were beheaded. Accusations pile up at the United Nations. You laugh at the president for the refusal to call out Islam as terrorist oriented. Peter Bergen of CNN laughs while pointing out that Osama bin Laden, the Saudi guerrilla/ financier and Taliban fellow traveler, an Islamo-maniac, was as filthy rich as folks like the Rockefellers. Meanwhile, bitter ole Rudy Giuliani approaches the birther point of view, saying the president, although patriotic, does not love America and was raised not to do so. As you would say, 'Jasus, ol' Rudy spent enough campaign money to support Alex Rodriguez for two baseball seasons and only got about one percent of the presidential primary votes. Who does not love whom, Rudy?' You love him, Wolf? Even McCain once defended the president when some nutty, typically ill-educated woman proclaimed our leader as a 'Moos-lim." However, you can't wait for the possible battle of Mosul, a gathering of, theoretically, forty thousand troops. Not quite a Gettysburg, but close."

Jen pauses and smiles. "There. Enough. Now tell me since it no longer matters. When and where do you plan to strike?"

Wolf smiles. "Well done, love. We are to it indeed. However, we need to lay out the stakes. When we finish, if you're good enough to figure it all out from clues and our game, you must be ready to decide how far you're willing to go to save yourself."

Once again thrown off guard, Jen does not respond.

Wolf adds. "Convert and convince me of it. If not, you get a last, late evening meal request, Red Lobster best we can do, and a last fuck in my arms, but only if it is consensual."

Silence as they stare into each other's eyes. Her Timex magnifies in her desperate imagination as loud as a bell tower.

CHAPTER TWENTY-ONE

Test and Trigger

Wolf levels his eyes at hers and begins. "One more thing, hon. Hand over the Timex and Mason diamond. You're clever enough to use that thing as a weapon to cut my throat."

Jen takes off the watch and ring, placing them on the table. Wolf pockets them and continues.

"You're convinced of two strikes. Granted. Now, what else are you certain about, anything?"

Jen meets his gaze. "I'm convinced you'll hit a government building with certainty the President will be in it. I think the first or second hit will be some sort of sports or entertainment venue, something with a huge crowd, including high-ranking members of our government."

Silence as Wolf gauges how to continue. He inhales deeply and speaks. "Not bad. Let's take those one at a time. What sporting event would draw the President and leaders with a huge crowd?"

Jen knows she has engaged him and knows he will allow it to evolve to full knowledge, signaling her conversion or death. She thinks and responds.

"Our man loves basketball but not enough people to satisfy your blood lust. Even if it were large enough, like an NBA All-Star game, not the kind of people you want to hit. You like sports too much to do it. Baseball on opening day might do but that means waiting a year. No way."

Wolf tilts his head and asks, "Therefore?"

"Entertainment, but I can't see the prez at a rock concert. I'd think theater, given your nasty remarks about show people and anecdotes over our interrogations, both by me and you."

Wolf nods. "You continue to impress, Jen, in so many ways. Think about the chat we had with famous names from entertainment."

Jen pauses, momentarily stopped cold. She wracks her brain trying to recall the blur of recent days. Nothing. She takes a wild guess.

"Arthur Miller? Monroe? Kazan?"

Wolf smiles. "Small clue. Dustin Hoffman." She suddenly recalls. "Tom Hanks."

Wolf nods. "Kool, honey, kool. Now use that good brain in your lovely head. Why in the world did we select who we did in that short game?"

Jen frowns and speaks cautiously. "Just favorites, I thought…"

She tapers off, then speaks firmly, "Wait. You actually offered clues about a strike!"

Wolf smiles but says nothing. Jen reflects. She asks herself silently. *What is a large enough venue to draw the President and many important people?*

After another hesitation, Wolf says quietly, "D.C. is loaded with symbolic locations, memorials, operative sites. Osama bin Laden had the right idea with 9/11 on many levels of influence, economic, political, AND symbolic."

Jen sighs and speaks, "Well, it wouldn't be any Memorial gathering, not enough people unless it was another March on Washington with a Martin Luther King."

She pauses, trying to see the city in her mind when

flying in or out of Washington. Finally she has it. "Ahh, of course, The Kennedy Center."

Wolf waits. She hesitates. He adds with a nod. "AND?"

The light bulb in her brain flashes. Every person in their exchange was honored by the President and important people at the Kennedy Center Awards in the Opera House Theater over the recent years. She speaks simply, almost foolishly.

"Yes. Huge venue."

Wolf smiles again. "Yes, and a very prominent cut of America is there with a gigantic public waiting to see it on national television. And the Man is there in evening dress."

Jen is with it now. "And very late in the year or early in the next. A perfect preliminary strike."

Wolf is grinning now in delight, pride. "Right, baby. A brand new leader the next day to prove again how the country rolls on. But not for long."

Jen actually feels faint, breathless. OF COURSE! is the phrase in her battered mind. She stares at him. He says nothing, leaning back in utter satisfaction. He is actually gloating in anticipation.

Finally Jen speaks. "You fool, the State of the Union night has the finest security ever assembled. If your Kennedy Center attack has a new President up there, even more security will be used! Outside, inside, in the air. No way."

Wolf chuckles aloud. "Really?"

Jen glares at him. "Even a plane or missile could never reach that target without interception."

He says, "No doubt, so what?"

Jen blinks and thinks. Her head lifts and she says. "I get it. Inside operatives. Has to be."

Now Wolf says nothing and does not move a muscle.

Jen continues. "Can't be. Anyone in the operation of both the Kennedy Center and Congress facilities has been so well vetted a fly couldn't slip through."

Wolf just remains silent and still.

Jen reflects, trying to think. Her head suddenly moves slightly right, then back at him slightly cocked to her right side. She almost whispers.

"Unless..."

Wolf widens his eyes innocently. "Unless?"

Jen replies, "Unless they've been there a very long time in very important positions and cleared of 'present danger' many times."

Wolf repeats, "AND?"

Jen concludes, trying to sound wise, not defeated. "And carefully recruited, converted over many carefully indoctrinated years. Plus big bucks."

Wolf stands up. He walks around the table behind her. He stops and asks a question with visceral intensity.

"What now, love, what now?"

Jen knows it is THE moment in this entire, frantic, dependent and dangerous relationship. She wonders to herself, How in hell did this actually become a relationship?

But it did and she knows it. She muses that she failed as Chief Interrogator. This son of a bitch was too much for her. Slowly, Jen stands to turn and face Wolf. Her burning final thought as she gets up is that she has one last chance to succeed, not for herself probably, but the country. Oddly her mind flashes not on beloved Dan, which he is, but beloved Smokey, which she is. Turning, Jen and Wolf are finally, intimately, close. They are not touching but their faces are inches apart.

Jen tries to soften her gaze, relax, show strength and conviction, not fear. The hummingbird confronts the wolf head on.

She speaks softly. "You know goddamn well I could never seriously convert. You'd never believe it if I tried."

Wolf's eyebrows raise in acknowledgement but he does not reply. He expected that kind of honesty. They are way past games and deception now. Only honesty serves in the eleventh hour. Indeed, it is late evening, past any notion of a last meal from Red Lobster. The mobile safe house has to be rolling with another hour or so.

Jen allows her mind to block out Dan, even Smokey, even the country and job she so loves. She looks into his eyes hoping to connect to—yes—desire.

In one final moment of mastery, Jen murmurs to him, "Turn the damn camera off in my compartment."

Swiftly Wolf pulls out his cell, hits a number, commands quietly, "Camera off in number three. Now, DO IT."

He drops the cell on the table, taking her into his arms. Human nature overcomes her last denial. Their eyes close as their lips meet.

CHAPTER TWENTY-TWO

Crisis and Climax

The passion was real for both of them, strong, stronger for him. He had wanted her from the start. She had known that but resisted any similar instinct because she was female and more powerful, willful. She had no other recourse than the plan she manipulated. He was a remarkable adversary in this as in everything, but he was male. She overcame his fine mind in the visceral domination of sexual desire.

Finally at the moment they struggled in their embrace into her compartment, disrobed, and fell onto her cot, she was in control and knew it. He just didn't care. His fatal flaw.

The passion sustained longer than either of them might have expected. Spent, he relaxes with such a shudder she flashes on how long it must have been for him. Perhaps he dozes. Perhaps he is just resting. His eyes are closed; he is motionless. She is no longer who she was minutes before. She is now a fully trained agent, armed and dangerous.

She had managed to grasp the weapon with the bra strap, dropping both bra and rigid straw as the final items on the floor next to the cot. The next question was could she reach the hardened straw with its deadly point without moving and waking him.

Sweaty seconds tick by but she grasps it. Before bringing her arm up, she deftly manipulates her fingers to firmly secure it in her right hand. The next step is to bring her right arm up into position without Wolf stirring. Done. The final move follows. Jen positions the weapon where her training told her is the precise spot on his neck to do full damage. Below his chin a fraction of an inch to the left. She is certain she will hit the carotid. With just a little extra luck, the twist might both muffle words and sound from the larynx, penetrating one or even both jugulars.

Jen inhales deeply, creating as much of the six pounds of thrusting pressure needed, tightens her grip on the weapon, pushes straight and hard as she can while exhaling, adding a fierce twist.

The skin never dimples. The tool smashes inward, striking two if not three arteries. Blood shoots out and down Jen's arm. Wolf's eyes shock fully open, his audible gasp is no scream. The dying struggle begins as his mind races into defensive action rather than any thought or words. His hands go to her neck but his strength is already waning. She manages to wrestle out of his grip, rolls on top of him, trying to pin his shoulders down. Blood gushes as his thrashing lessens.

A gurgling sound emits from his lips with blood and saliva. In no more than a minute or two, his eyes set as final breath rolls out of his body next to her left cheek. Her face relaxes limply above the wound as though in a final embrace.

For an instant Jen is frozen. Her mind clicks back to the reality of action. Their thrashing may have been heard. Actually, she hopes so, moving naked to the hinged side of the small door. She positions herself for the hardest Tae Kwon Do move possible from her black belt days.

Rahm dashes into the compartment, a .45 automatic

in his left hand. He sees Wolf, instinctively racing to him. A mistake. Jen collapses him with a wicked blow to the back of his neck. He falls, the .45 dropping onto Wolf's chest. Jen reaches in a flash, grabs the pistol, fires a shot into the back of Rahm's skull. She wheels around, expecting Ahmed to be there but he is not.

She hides again by her compartment door until she hears Ahmed running. Adroitly, expertly, her field training snaps in again. Jen drops to one knee in the opening of her door, firing automatically into the dead center of that next doorway. Ahmed is indeed in the middle of that door, his .45 pistol in hand. Jen's shot hits him flush in the stomach.

He emits a howl, dropping to his knees.

Jen fires another shot as she rises, striking him over his right eye. He drops dead in the doorway.

Silence.

At the far rear of the trailer, Faisal is immobile, silent, knowing three shots have been fired, leaving him alone in sudden stillness. His .45 is in hand but he has to decide on fight or flight.

The experienced driver has had almost no real field training as an ISIS warrior. No killer, he opts for flight. Jen is standing in her own doorway looking toward the rear of the trailer, poised and ready to kill a fourth time. Had she stopped to realize that fact she might have frozen or trembled.

Faisal leaps to the large metal doors, slams down the latch, preparing to open it and leap to safety. Jen fires again, aiming perfectly, hitting her target in the back of his right thigh. Faisal drops in pain, groaning, the .45 dangling for a moment, then dropping to the floor.

Unaware she is still as naked as the day she was born, Jen races to him, kicking his pistol away. Spotting some packing straps in the corner, she quickly puts a tourniquet around Faisal's leg, then locks his hands behind him.

Trained for capture, Faisal says nothing.

Finally, full awareness of the past few minutes flushes over Jen. Only a few minutes have transpired since her plan began. She walks to her compartment to splash water from the sink faucet over her face, arms, and hands. She towels briefly, retrieves her clothing, and dresses.

As she finishes by stepping into her shoes and tying the laces, she hears sirens. Good, she thinks, the police will give her a phone to call the Bureau, then Dan. She inhales deeply and briefly checks the pulse on Wolf. She reaches into his pocket, retrieving her ring and watch.

She checks the pulse of Rahm and Ahmed.

Jen heads to the rear of the trailer. Only Faisal is breathing, moaning softly as she walks toward him, thinking, He'll end up telling us the rest of this story but not quickly enough.

Jen knows the two D.C. buildings that need immediate personnel vetting. Spotting the small case she uses rather than a purse, she opens it. Her metal FBI identifying pin is attached to the inside cover of the case. She retrieves it, then grabs her cell. It is dead, of course.

She pushes open the large metal doors at the back of the trailer. Several Staunton, Virginia, police officers in riot gear are looking at her, weapons poised, looking terrified. Jen raises her right hand with the FBI pin saying, "Code Jen, FBI. Someone help me down and loan me a phone."

CHAPTER TWENTY-THREE

Shift and Settle

It takes only one phone transfer at Hoover for Jen to reach the man himself, the FBI Director. She humbly brushes aside his praise to tell him briefly about the two strikes. The Director does not wait beyond learning the names of the two facilities and Jen's hunch to check on both engineering and security personnel without delay. They both knew this has to be done with haste before news gets out to the public about what had just gone down. Jen hands the cell back to the police sergeant, leaning back to rest a moment in the squad car and think.

An ambulance departs with Faisal for a hospital, two policemen in attendance. Another unmarked van is backed up to the trailer truck. Jen watches as three body bags are lifted down, then placed in the van. She is relieved to see two more officers climb into the van as it speeds off toward the morgue.

At this point, another officer opens the door beside her in the squad car, handing her an object. It's a cold bottle of clear, La Croix sparkling drinking water. The can is open. She drinks, the carbonation smarting her eyes.

The policeman speaks. "Our medic just arrived. They want you over to his vehicle for a preliminary check."

Jen nods and says, "Give me five. One more important call."

Dan is joyous but starts asking questions. She explains she cannot talk now. She repeats that she is unharmed, promising she will see him tomorrow, noting where she is but giving no hint of what she has managed or how.

Walking to the medical van, she finally begins to chill, almost tremble.

Her blood pressure is being taken by a nice looking doctor in his forties. He has a greying mustache. The small silver badge on his white jacket reads 'Dr. Travis Arias.' Looking up to his face, she meets his dark blue eyes. He is not a dead ringer for the traitor she just killed but close enough. Her memory fires to the look in Wolf's eyes at the moment his arteries burst. A sweeping nausea slams through Jen's body, bile coursing through her throat into her mouth. She jerks away from the poor doctor, vomiting hideously over the small table holding medical equipment.

She slips to her knees on the floor of the ambulance, retching over and over. The doctor and his young Hispanic attendant, Marie, try to assist, but Jen collapses full out on the floor, lapsing into dry heaves. Utterly dehydrated, exhausted. Her body finally relaxes. She is unconscious.

CHAPTER TWENTY-FOUR

Surge and Sweep

Jen awakens in a medivac helicopter, whirring north toward D.C. A tube in her arm extends upward to a bag dripping fluid. A new doctor and a nurse are on each side of her. Jen is lying in a collapsed gurney.

The doctor sees her eyes open and asks, "Feeling better? You were very sick."

Jen replies, "Yes, thank you. Where are we going?"

The doctor glances at the nurse, then answers, "The Staunton medics wanted to hospitalize you, of course. The Director vetoed that, needing you in D.C. asap. He said to tell you there are rapid developments."

Jen tries to sit up but the doctor shakes his head, placing his hands on her shoulders. She does not resist but asks another question.

"How long was I out?"

The doctor shrugs. "You actually went into what we determined was mild shock. We've been in the air fifteen minutes or so."

He glances out a window. "D.C. dead ahead." He hands her a paper cup. "Hot tea, it'll help. You need food. They reopened the heliport for this. We'll be on the roof of the Hoover Building in minutes. Soup and croissants with the Director."

He smiles and turns away, adding, "He must be very grateful to you." Jen finds the tea too bitter but not so hot she cannot drink it all.

As she does so, the iron bird waffles into a landing. The doctor removes the drip from her arm, wrapping an elastic blue binding around the slightly bruised point where the needle was inserted. Two agents are waiting for her with a wheelchair which she waves off.

In five minutes Jen is seated across from the Director and a man she does not know. The chicken noodle soup is there, steaming, along with a large croissant, accompanied by two pads of butter and two small containers of grape jelly. The mind does strange things. She wishes it were orange marmalade. However, she dives in at the Director's urging.

As she eats, also relishing the glass of cold milk, the Director introduces the stranger. "This is Tom Drake, Gordon replacement," He smiles wryly and adds, "Better vetted than the fucking traitor."

Jen puts down her spoon to shake Drake's hand, but he waves her off with a smile. "Chow down, Code Jen, chow." They all chuckle and relax.

The Director lights a pipe with a lovely aroma and speaks. "Jen, in those sessions with Wolf, did you ever hear the names, Pasha Quresh and Abdul Wissa?"

Jen replies, "No, sir."

The Director continues. "Pasha's a heating and cooling engineer at the Kennedy Center office below the Opera House Theater. Abdul's the same position in Congress, directly below the chamber where the President gives the State of the Union address. The names just leaped out at us, of course."

Jen cannot help but interrupt. "My God, do they know? THEY'LL RUN!" The Director holds up a hand.

"Relax. No news releases yet. Both men in custody.

They were asleep. Their families are bewildered—under watch and care. The two men are in full denial. They're long-time employees, well vetted, impeccable records. A very deep cell, as good as we've seen. 'Wolf West' had to be some sort of genius. He converted, trained them. He was charismatic, brilliant, utterly captivating, persuasive. Well, you interrogated, I'm telling you nothing you don't know in spades."

That barrage of words about the man jars her. She nearly chokes on the last of the croissant. She finishes the milk, trying to find a reply. She can only sigh.

Jen slightly alters the subject. "Stunning work, sir, congratulations."

The Director quickly responds, "We have you to thank. You're going to get a good physical, then a well-earned vacation."

Jen's organized thinking kicks into gear. "When do I have to submit my report?"

A short pause follows, the Director is slightly surprised that she seems so disciplined under the circumstances. He shrugs. "That can wait 'til after the physical. We certainly look forward to every detail. Frankly, Jen, we haven't a clue how you pulled that off. You eliminated the core of the cell. Now we have the two, key insiders. They'll break if only for the sake of their families."

He is grinning ear to ear. "Jen we nailed one major bonus."

Jen inhales and asks, "There's more?"

The Director turns to Drake. "Tell her, Tom."

Tom eagerly responds. "Pasha and Abdul separately asked for the same attorney! One Ashram Saade of a major legal firm in Arlington. We checked him out, smelling money plus plenty of Middle East connections. We had him under watch anyway, but this all made too much sense to be a coincidence."

The Director continues the account. "Jen, we picked

him up shortly after the two engineers asked for him. When he came to the door of his palatial mansion in Arlington, he was furious that they had given his name. Major fuckup there. He's undoubtedly the funding source for this cell, a successful real estate attorney."

Jen chuckles. "They fucked up by never expecting the engineers to be identified, arrested, never told them who to call or not call."

Tom adds, "Right. Shocked at the arrest, in a panic, they knew they needed legal help. Ashram leaped to mind. It won't matter now; we'll put them all away. ISIS leaders will want them dead one way or another."

Jen thinks about the one living Muslim. "What about Faisal, the one I wounded, the driver."

The Director nods. "We'll see what we can get from him. Tom will interrogate himself."

Tom adds, "Yes, but, Jen, I want you with me, Together, we can break this one fast."

It is at that moment when some lingering, buried thought, steeped in fearful enlightenment, thrusts into her mind. Words scream in her head. *NO MORE! NO MORE! FINISHED!*

Her silence is awkward. The Director senses everything is moving too rapidly for this agent who just went through the trauma of a lifetime. He quickly breaks the silence.

"Well, that will be up to you, Jen, no rush. Right now, we want to get you checked out. Then a nice break, rest. I talked to Dan. He'll get time off from V.A. counseling and join you."

As Jen meets the medical team waiting for her outside the Director's office, her head is swimming again. The elevator descends to the basement and waiting ambulance. All she can think about is the report.

The idea of detailing in writing what happened, in the required FBI detail, sears her heart.

As the ambulance roars into the street, siren wailing,

Jen forces her mind to one thing: hummingbirds.

CHAPTER TWENTY-FIVE

Flutter and Fly

After dinner at Notti Bianche, Jen, Dan, and Smokey go to her apartment in Georgetown for a glass of sherry.

Jen makes it clear from the start that what she has experienced has shaken her to her core. Dan wisely intuits she is not ready to have him stay the night as though nothing had happened to her. However, that fact in itself prompts a serious discussion. Dan begins by asking what he thinks is his most serious question.

"I gathered from the Director there was a shoot-out in that truck. I know you weren't wounded. May I ask how many terrorists held you captive?"

Jen is speechless, ready to beg off questions so soon. Yet, she understands his misery, what he has also been through.

Dan continues. "Must I wait for the report? Worse yet, television news? I've avoided everything til I saw you!"

Jen looks at this dear man, suffering worse somehow than she is. She responds.

"There were four. I managed to create a weapon. I terminated three of them, wounded the other."

The silence is crippling. His eyes water. She continues.

"I'm going to need some time, a break, vacation. You

and Smokey will be with me. I may be able to tell you more in time. I may not."

For several seconds Jen stares at her sherry, saying nothing. She looks up. Dan is silently weeping. Her heart is breaking. Knowing he needs to more, she bravely, compassionately, resumes.

"There were three Muslims, respectful, did nothing to me. The lead American you knew as the pungent smelling one." That remark relieves the tension a bit. Dan inhales, the tears gone. He asks another question.

"Was that the entire cell?"

Jen grasps the questions with relief. She did not have to say more about Wolf. She answers quickly.

"There were three others. Our agents grabbed two key plants in target buildings soon after I relayed the information I'd obtained."

Jen races on to avoid having to explain the 'games,' the mad exchanges, all that she learned and how.

"The Bureau was at their best, Dan. They got the wealthy funding source, too. All seven men in the cell were Muslims except for the American turncoat."

Dan hesitates to continue, but he cautiously does so. "Jen, I know you were trained to defend yourself with deadly force if necessary. I realize this was necessary. I also know that will take some time, perhaps therapy, to overcome. You must have been through what almost no one ever faces in life."

There is an awful silence for a moment. Her eyes are full of tears but she cannot speak. This sightless man senses her anguish. He continues.

"I admit to you as the man who loves you and will stand by you forever, marriage or not, I naturally would like to know just how you managed a weapon in that dreadful situation. Can you tell me that much?"

Jen knows Dan is suffering from sheer fearful imagination. She inhales, replies.

"I made a weapon. I used what little was available to me. My training prepared me for it, though not for the weapon I was able to devise. I ask you in return not to ask me more than that fact. It's bad enough to have reconstruct it all in the report I must write tomorrow."

Dan sighs and nods. "I see."

Jen continues. "I know you have a desire, perhaps a right, to know more. If you push for it, I'll break a rule. You can read the report before I turn it in. I wish you wouldn't, but it's up to you."

Dan stares at her. His admiration and love for this woman remain solid; but, he senses great upheaval if he pushes this further. He smiles and speaks. He knows the courage it took for her to make that offer. He knows she will comply if he asks. Some intangible sense of decency in him prompts him to take a higher road.

"Jen, I will not need to read the report. I'll pursue this no further."

Jen's entire being relaxes. "Thank you, Dan. You're the strongest person I've ever known."

She leans forward and kisses him. She adds softly, her forehead resting on his. "No one but you, what you've been through, could be so compassionate, let alone love me as you do."

Dan senses a finality about their relationship in terms of marriage, but also senses a security about their love and future. He thinks to himself, life partners will do. With The Poot too, of course.

Jen pours them a refill of sherry, shocking him with her next remark. "After the report, I think I'll resign. Call it early retirement."

Silence. They sip the sherry. Finally, Dan speaks quietly. "That bad, wow." He pauses. "Yes. I understand. However, think clearly. You're young. What would you do, get a job as a secretary? Back to school? What?"

He has caught her up short. She obviously has not

thought this through beyond the report and resignation.

Jen responds. "Okay, you got me. For now. I don't know yet, but I'll figure it out."

Dan offers the only truth available. "Fair enough. I think you'll change your mind. Whatever, I'm with you all the way, if you want me to be."

She looks at him a moment, finding that truth. "I want you with me all the way. Pootie too."

They embrace. He and Pootie gather themselves together, departing for their apartment, Dan insisting on catching a taxi, declining a ride in the Mustang.

Alone at last, Jen puts away the sherry. She knows she will write the report in full detail, honestly, no holds barred. She knows she will tender her resignation. She knows the Director will decline to accept it. He will ask her to keep it until after the vacation with Dan and Pootie in Tucson. Long walks near Mt. Lemmon, strolling among the Saguaros in the desert heat will mix with good swims, good food, good drinks.

She knows damn well she will tear up the resignation. She will find the strength to do only what she can do. Jen will continue her career, for now with the Bureau. Beyond that, who knows?

Jen sleeps fitfully. In a dream just before waking, a man in a white coat tells her she is pregnant. Jen awakes with a start, perspiring, the room in total darkness. Her mind races, My God, life from Wolf inside me? She forces a hollow laugh, shudders, rises, and showers. She willfully dismisses the dream, remembering her hummingbird. She starts to sing to keep her mind on the day ahead. Getting to know you, getting to know all about.... She stops in mid-verse, turns off the shower, and freezes for a moment before reaching for a large beach towel from the Capri Hotel in Laguna Beach.

At first sunlight, she is in her small kitchen sipping a Starbucks Veranda blonde blend. Looking out her window, she sees that she still has not refilled the hummingbird feeder.

At that moment, a small familiar hummingbird appears, hovers, and sees the still empty container. In an instant, she flies away.

Jen lifts the coffee cup, the heat rising into her fading smile. She takes a careful sip as tears drop into the shimmering brew, sending ripples toward the edges of the old chipped cup.

THE END

ABOUT THE AUTHOR

Jerry L. Crawford, a native Iowan, went from a one-room elementary, country schoolhouse without electricity and plumbing to a small high school of fifty students, thence to Drake University for a B.F.A. in Acting, an M.A. in Directing from Stanford University, and a Ph.D. in Playwriting from The University of Iowa. He is a two-year veteran of the United States Army. He then taught for thirty-two years at the University of Nevada, Las Vegas, heading the acting and directing program prior to founding the MFA program in Playwriting. Crawford served fifteen summers as Director of Literary Seminars and advisor to the Plays in Progress program at the Utah Shakespeare Festival. He also served at UNLV for three years as Dean of Faculty. Commensurate with his service there, he spent four different years on Sabbatical in New York City as a professional playwright represented by Robert A. Freedman Dramatic Agency, Inc.

He was a resident playwright at The Actors Studio, Circle Repertory Company, and the Hartman Theatre, with his plays done in theaters in Edinburgh, Baltimore, Akron, Las Vegas, Fresno, Stockton, Cedar City, Indianapolis, Missosula, Helena, Lawrence, and Baton Rouge, among others. Author of thirty-six plays, a novel in play form, and *Past Light*, a memoir, *Torpor* is his first novella. Winner of many awards as actor, director and writer, he is author of the text, *Acting in Person and In Style*, 5th edition, Waveland Press. Crawford spent over twenty years as theater critic around the country for the American College Theater Festival and The American Community Theater

Association. He served in national roles of leadership for ACTF.

Crawford is Dean Emeritus of The College of Fellows of the American Theater at the Kennedy Center. In his retirement, he is also known as a film critic under the banner, "YOOPER CRITIC SEES..." He is currently Adjunct Professor of Theater and English at Northern Michigan University. A lifelong fan of the Cleveland Indians, he traveled twice with the team through spring training as a sports journalist assisting famed sports writers, Terry Pluto and Sheldon Ocker.

His wife of fifty-five years, Patricia, passed in 2011. He has a son, two daughters, and five grandchildren. Crawford is currently working on a new comedy for the theater, *The Deal*. He is aided in this by his faithful and talented dog, Foo Foo.